# True Colors-the accidental heist

## Story

Clive Dev

## Chief Editor

Ashamole Clive

# Clive Dev

This is a work of fiction. Names, characters, businesses, places, events, locales and incidents are either the products of the author's imagination or used in a fictitious manner. Any resemblance to actual persons, living or dead, or actual events is purely coincidental.

**OTHER BOOKS BY Clive Dev**

- **THE PROMISE BETWEEN US – Detective Dev Crime Thriller Series**

- **STRANGERS INSIDE - Detective Dev Crime Thriller Series**

- **SOME GOOD HEARTS STILL ..........-Romance (short story kindle edition)**

**COMING SOON**

- **THREADS OF LIFE - The turbulence**

*Clive Dev*

## Chapter 1: September 13th ;19:00

Situated on the cliffs on the coast of Hayabala, this building was very gigantic. The perimeter wall was a majestic brick red which stood about one hundred feet tall and ten feet wide. Spread over an area of fifty acres, the ground was covered with a concrete floor. The walls of the inner building were made of grey cement. A contrast to the outer wall which provided a sense of beauty; this grey lifeless wall was the true facade of the building. The walls were as grey as the life of the prisoners inside it was drab. Yes, this was a prison!

A heavily guarded fortress to keep inside the men, who had committed serious offences against the general public. Also, the men who had committed small crimes against powerful influential people were incarcerated here. No one could escape this prison. It was not internationally reputed for its safety; neither did the management boast of its iron clad security. The inmates who tried and lost their lives in the process were the undeniable evidence. The convicts who tried and lived, swore never to do it again. They cannot even if they want to now. A taste of an unsuccessful death; supplies you with the agony of a life time.

On one side was a heavily guarded woodland and the other three sides were the rocky cliffs stretching up to a kilometre into the North Atlantic Ocean. Although the rocky cliffs were constantly washed by the waters of the Atlantic, an attempt by anyone to dive into the ocean from the brick wall of the prison will be a death wish come true. There was only one way in and out!

Inside the compound was the living quarters for the correction officers. They could live with their family if they wished. The enclosure also housed a gymnasium which helped tap into the testosterone in these men. It was important to burn off the excess energy that came from the rich luxurious food cooked in the modern kitchen at the back of the cottage. The men ate in the dining area attached to the kitchen while on duty. The gym also helped to keep the men energetic, fresh and out of trouble. An all-male work force runs the risk of reducing the sense of decorum in the men. This is human psychology. We unconsciously behave better in the presence of the opposite sex. The families who live there, will not be seen anywhere near the main building of the prison. They lived in a separate mini world behind the red brick wall.

The outer wall had a large gate which was always guarded by a team of three prison officers. The two guard dogs were held on a tight leash during the day and were let loose during the night. The prison officers and the dogs shared the comparatively small 'cottage' which was just inside the huge wall.

It was no ordinary hut! It was a concrete building equipped with CCTV, motion sensors and emergency flood lights. These lights mounted on the walls, revolved around the perimeter of the building and flooded the place with light at all times. The lights were set in such a manner, that the brightness emanating from these bulbs covered every inch of the floor space and each of the three hundred and sixty degree at any given time. There was no blind spot. Unlike any ordinary systems this was solar operated with batteries that had large storage capacity. The bulbs were set to react to the day light. This meant that if ten in the morning was cloudy, the lights turned on automatically. No room for human error here!

The central office had a CCTV monitoring station with ten computers and a visual display unit. Each VDU had ten sub screens which received images from ten cameras. Each VDU was under the scrutiny of one person. The overhead cameras in this room observed the activity of the men watching the monitors. Each person was responsible for the area that was visible on their screen. Again, there was no blind spot; the cameras on all the four sides were set to revolve clockwise; so, the ground was completely covered between them.

A mobile battalion made up of a team of three officers covered the grounds including the woodland on a jeep equipped with sophisticated instruments. There were five such battalions covering the perimeter at any one time. One shift comprised of thirty men on duty and the duration of the beat was six hours. This meant that fresh pairs of eyes and feet worked on the beat at all times. Because of this rotation, tiredness was no excuse in this place. These prisoners were all very high profile and were meant to be locked away.

There was no senior officer in this group. They all led the team in rotation. Each man got the experience to cook, clean, lead and exercise judgement equally. The leader for the day got the hand over for the last twenty-four hours shift. He then, reported to the prison warden

Stone but also, had the autonomy to make day to day decisions.

A beautifully kept garden in the corner of the prison grounds looked like an oasis in the middle of the desert. The kitchen garden was the nearest to the building and the fruit garden was on the opposite side. Both gardens were circular in design and the flower garden occupied the intersection between the two circles. The fruit trees were planted very far apart in the perimeter of the garden. So, the line of vision was always clear. Prisoners with green fingers were allowed to work in this place. This was a coveted job as these inmates were the only ones, who got more fresh air and sunshine when compared to the others. In addition to the possession of green fingers, you had to prove your worth to get this job.

There was a rotation system where no prisoner could become familiar with the other. However, in a confined space, familiarity cannot be avoided. Long term prisoners were known to each other and forged an informal bond in small groups. This was grudgingly accepted by the correction officers as there was only so much isolation that could be maintained. Man is a social animal and will always lean towards forming a group. This was an inherent characteristics that helped with survival of the species. For the prisoners to be put into solitary confinement; there has to be a threat to the inmate's and the officer's lives. Apart from the occasional skirmishes, this lot were harmless!

The cattle shed was at the back of the prison and the cattle were free to roam the perimeter. Each animal was armed with a tracking device which kept them safe and accounted for. The correction officers were the ones who minded the cattle and made the prisoners work in these sheds. This was considered the most tedious job. The inmates on-duty in the cattle farm, had to manually milk the cows before dawn. This meant that, they had to wake up at four in the morning and clean the animals and the stalls first. They hated mucking in the cattle dung. Everyone was put on rotation for this job regardless of their chosen vocation.

A camera fitted drone was also flying around; within the perimeter of the campus and provided live feed to the officers inside the monitoring room. They had two drones which were kept fully charged at all times. At present the 'on-duty' drone was at a height of fifty meters above the wall and the officer could see a police car driving up the woodland road that fed into the access road to the prison. "So, they were getting a new inmate!" the person watching that camera in the CCTV room thought to himself. Only the group leader for the day will be aware of the arrival of a potential inmate. This meant that, the officers at the gate were never complacent about who approached the area.

The police car drew up to the prison gates. The dogs began to bark madly. The prison officer who was in-charge of the dogs was struggling very hard to restrain the animals. The prison officer at the gate, went to the vehicle and acknowledged the police officers in the car. He had a good look at the inside of the car with a practiced eye. He saw two officers and one prisoner who was handcuffed. The other officer checked under the body of the car with a telescopic inspection mirror. Once satisfied, the third officer opened the gate and allowed the police car to drive through.

The main building had a custody office at the entrance where the prisoners were processed before being admitted into the system. This office had two rooms. One was a camera room where the prisoner's pictures were taken. The second room was the administration unit where the documents were stored, case reports were made; and the prisoner's rehabilitation plan was determined and completed. This prisoner was processed in three hours which is the minimum. This convict seems to be low risk!

Once processed, the prisoner was brought to a cell where he was doubled up with another inmate. The already resident inmate was Pablo, a Spanish guy who was imprisoned for second degree felony. He mentally measured up the new inmate. 'Harmless' was the verdict he gave to the new arrival. Pablo had seen a lot of prisoners in his years of confinement. He was able to now discern at one glance, the level of cruelty a prisoner was capable of. The officer who escorted the prisoner, left the cell block. He had handed over the induction pack to the new arrival. The prisoner had plenty of 'time' to read it!


Pablo looked at this stranger. He in return eyed him as well. After some hesitation, he smiled. "Hello, my name is Mark." Pablo hesitated for a few seconds. Then, he extended his hand to Mark with a smile and introduced himself. He also informed Mark that he had arrived to a model prison which was considered to be a real privilege. They got on well within the first few minutes. He advised Mark to cover his tattoo with the sleeve of his uniform; dinner time was near and he will be targeted in the dining room. "You will be standing out like a beacon," Mark listened to Pablo's advice with intense concentration and thanked him.


Once Mark was ready, they both walked to the dining area. Mark took a deep breath as he prepared to face the crowd. Since he was convicted for the first time, he was way out of his depth here. He looked around the dining area in apprehension. The room had many sets of tables with six chairs. Each table was occupied by one or two people. There was a queue of inmates lined up at the food counter. They were being served by the senior inmates who worked in the kitchen on a rotational basis. Mark copied Pablo's activities. He had become his mentor and guide by default. They joined the queue.

A sudden violent movement heralded the arrival of a notorious prisoner. He pushed Mark and then, Pablo. The correction officer watching this encounter smacked his baton on the table. "Quiet," he ordered. Antonio looked at Mark's reaction. He was satisfied. Mark was shocked but Pablo was prepared. He held Mark's hand in restrain. There was a note of caution in his eyes. Mark kept his mouth shut.

He looked at Pablo in pain. He was sucked out of his breath by the unexpected assault. Once the earthquake called Antonio and his cronies, the aftershocks had gone to the top of the line, Pablo whispered to Mark about the nature of this guy. "He is the bully of the prison. The correction officers turn a blind eye to many of his antics. Only reason being that he does not provoke a lot of people at any given time".

Antonio moved to the head of the queue and pushed back all the people who were ahead of him at the top of the line. A hand belonging to the person behind him landed softly on his shoulder. Antonio braced his shoulder and discretely elbowed the person in the stomach. The inmate who got the unpleasant punch, folded over in pain. He breathed out his pain through clenched teeth. Antonio looked back at him and grinned widely. The inmate smiled through his pain but, his eyes were moist.

All the prisoners have to collect their food and walk quietly to their own table. This is the rule of the dining room. Antonio left the queue after collecting his food. But he stopped by another table and chatted to some other inmate. Then he moved over to his table and sat down. He faced his friend who was already seated and was deep in conversation.

Antonio's fork suddenly fell to the floor. It seemed that in his hurry to speak to his friend; he had not kept the fork properly on the plate. He looked down and bent over to pick up his fork. A strong knee connected with Antonio's chin brutally. His head strikes up to the heavy table reflexively and makes a loud banging noise. The double impact from the table at the top and Jason's knee at the bottom makes

Antonio speechless. He looks up. Jason was looking down and grinning at him. "You are being rewarded for the good deeds you did on your way down" he said. Antonio suddenly got up from his table in a rage but, he saw a correction officer walk towards them.

Each one of them are aware of the consequences of attracting the attention of the correction officers so, Antonio also decided to desist. God only knows how that was possible? But Antonio maintained silence. He knew that he will be in trouble along with Jason. They might be adversaries, but they were blood brothers and held here for the same reason. To be kept away from society. He cannot let the officer have the pleasure of punishing them more. He will get an opportunity on another day. Jason is conscious of Antonio at his back, but he is confident that he will keep quiet for now. He knows that Antonio will wait for a suitable moment; it most probably will be the recreation room. He continued to walk up to his table.

His four friends; who were already seated there, had seen the encounter. They grinned in acknowledgement to Jason's smile. The correction officers were watching all of this. They only interfered if the violence was going to escalate into a group war. They knew that this skirmish is over for tonight.

Jason went and sat in his chair. His friends patted him on his shoulder. Antonio was still glaring at him. Brady was the first one to acknowledge him. "You taught him a good lesson.  He is probably seeing stars at the moment". Jason turned around and looked at Antonio. He laughed heartily in the pure pleasure of seeing Antonio's face screwed in pain. "You know Brady! That was the highlight of the day" he replied to his friend and cellmate.

Jimmy leaned over towards Jason. "Jason, you are right. "an eye for an eye and a tooth for a tooth'. He needed it desperately." David who was on Jason's left and across from him whispered softly. "Jason, he will pay you back for this; you know that?" Jason replied. "Of course, David! I know that. But I will still do it. I will pay him back on the double, if he even looked at any of you with an evil intention." Lucas who never could say a good word but never wanted to be left behind, piped in. "Yeah, right no one is that sincere here; to actually take the slack for the other." David glared at him. He was fed up with his brother always being negative about his friends. Jason looked at Lucas pointedly but refused to be drawn into that debate.

Hearing this interaction would make one think that they were bosom buddies; that was not the case at all. They had all met here in this same prison. The length of their sentence had brought on this camaraderie and over time, they had become very fond of each other. Jason who is officially Jason Jazz is serving the longest sentence of fifteen years. That made him the senior most member of this group. He was younger than Brady and Jimmy in age. But they always looked up to him for his level headedness and his charisma. He was cool and suave as well.

Jason was convicted with the possibility of Parole. He was sentenced for seizing two million dollars from a single armoured van burglary. He got caught because his car stalled on the highway. The police thought of him as a one-man army who worked for himself. His policy was, that it made it easier to escape from the law; if he had no connections.

Brady was a car thief. Not an ordinary car thief; he always went for the most expensive cars. Lamborghini, Aston Martin and Ferrari were his favourites. The richer the owner, the more thrill he felt in his handiwork. This meant he also got caught very quickly. He never stole the car for money. He stole them for the adrenaline rush that occurred with the theft. He exulted in the challenge that came with breaking every modern automobile security system. The county judge got fed up with him and put him behind bars for a good ten years. He had connections with a lot of gangsters. A small time robber committing a small crime and when caught will always pass on information to the police in exchange for a better deal. That is how he always got caught. Brady had a wife, now ex and has a child. A boy, whom he had not seen since coming in to the prison. The boy was six years old at the time. A very impressionable age!

Jimmy whose full name was James Hartigan, was a fan of using proverbs and quotes. He was a computer hacker and had mis appropriated the finances of many multinational, national, large and small corporate companies. He has received ten years for his crime. Now, the millions he stole were resting in the state treasury. He has no connections, family or friends outside of this place. He was a loner.

David Kowalski was a 6 foot tall Polish guy who was a forensic expert. He was the most serious natured and straight forward person in the group. He got mixed up with robbers and gang lords because, they had threatened him with his parents' life.

They wanted him to change the evidence in their favour and he did it for the sake of his parents' safety. It is a known truth that if you yield to their demand once, you will always remain in their clutches. His latest venture was to change the evidence for a robbery at a famous jewellery merchant's establishment. He got caught by his colleague who suspected him of unrighteous deeds for some time. He got a prison sentence of ten years.

Lucas is David's twin. He became a member of this group by association. He was a gun maker and had worked in the government arms and ammunitions factory. All humans have an evil streak in them. It lies buried deep inside them somewhere. The righteous nature is the dominant personality in ninety percent of the population in the world. Lucas' holy side slowly got weaker and weaker. His evil side when it became dominant; made him decide that he could make more money by going private.

He began to supply his expertise to drug lords and gangsters. The quality of arms and ammunitions he made; was better than what the government ammunitions factory churned out. He got caught when he was delivering a consignment of illegally made weapons and landed in prison for twelve years. He is the least favoured person in this group.

Jason looked at each one of them and remarked soberly that all, except him; were leaving for the outside world the next day. He will be on his own. Brady looked at him with anxiety and said that he was really worried being out there after such a long time. Jason reassured Brady that, he will be fine and advised, "Just be on good behaviour till I get out". Everyone except for Lucas laughed. Lucas dryly remarked that Jason will not be getting out any time soon.

David is really annoyed at him now and admonished him to keep quiet. "Lucas can you mind your words please? You are a member of the group by virtue of being my little brother". Lucas gives back for good measure to his twin. He was annoyed that he was siding with his friends instead of his brother. "Yeah? Thanks for the support."

David reminded him that prison life for Lucas was made easy because of Jason's reputation. Jimmy admonished them both to keep quiet as the guards were directly observing them now. Brady turned towards Jason, "Jason, regardless of Lucas' nature; what he is saying is correct. I am going to miss you terribly." Jason reassured Brady, "Don't worry pal, I will be out in next month's parole hearing." He secretly hoped that he will be successful. The men all went back to their individual cells in response to the bell announcing the end of the dinner time.

Mark and Pablo were back in their cell after dinner and were seated on their own beds across from each other. Mark is still in pain from the unexpected attack from Antonio. Pablo looked at him with sympathy and told him that he will have to learn to keep quiet. "Do you see people separate two animals when they are fighting with each other?" Mark looked up at him in surprise and nodded his head, "No, why?" Pablo answered, "It is the same in the prison. Prison officers never separate two fighting men unless it gets out of hand". These were the realities of prison life. If someone decided to do something about it, they were discovered by the inmates themselves and punished them for being a telltale and a 'rat'. The 'lights off' bell could be heard which ended Mark and Pablo's conversation. They switched off the lights and lay down to sleep. Each drifted into their own world of loneliness.

## Chapter 2: September 14ᵗʰ 11:00

The morning air was cold, crisp and fresh. The day was sunny. Brady, Jimmy, David and Lucas stood outside the prison gates. They had been officially released. They had said their goodbyes to Jason after breakfast. David and Lucas' parents were waiting with their car outside the prison gate. They were anxious and wanted to get away from there as quickly as possible. However, Lucas and David took their time bidding farewell to the other two.

David shook his hand with Brady and Jimmy. 'Well, this is it. Our parents are waiting. I am surprised that they are here at all". Jimmy laughed and remarked "Perhaps they think that you have turned over a new leaf." Lucas grunted in response. David and Lucas walked up to their parents and hugged them. They got into the car, waved good bye to their now friends and ex-prison mates and drove off.


Jimmy turned towards Brady and reiterated his offer of sharing his home. Brady without sounding ungrateful refused and thanked him just as he had previously. "I know, and I will come and find you if I am stuck. We have been living in each other's hair for too long". Jimmy understood the feeling. He knew if they shared accommodations; the feeling of prison life will still be there. He did not want that either; but, he just wanted to help out his brethren in need. Jimmy extended his hand to Brady "Well then." Brady shook hands with Jimmy and they both parted ways. Jimmy got into the waiting taxi and left.


Brady slowly walked through the woodland. He breathed in the fresh air and slowly came to grips with his freedom. He kept walking at a slow pace to the small town which was a good few kilometers away from the prison. He took his time. He had nowhere to go. No one was waiting for him. He will look for accommodations for tonight with the money earned in the prison. He will begin to look for work tomorrow. His parole officer had met him yesterday and had made a few suggestions. He will suss those places out. It took him a couple of hours to get out of the woods surrounding the prison. As he walked to the edge of the woodlands, he saw a few buildings that had cropped up over the years he had spent indoors. Well, it was a good few years and time waits for no one.

He looked around at all the houses with its large double gates. Sure enough the land was pretty cheap here. The houses and their back gardens were huge. "What do you expect? Even the land around the prison will carry a stigma" he thought to himself. Living near a prison is a potential threat to people's lives and a suspicion on the resident's morality and their character. Moreover, there was a cemetery on the left side of the road. That would have doubled the people's fear. It is only the very brave, who will live beside a cemetery. Brady walked on the footpath. He was flanked by the road on one side and a small strip of grassland on the other. These were a good distance from the houses.

As he walked further, he saw a man sitting on the grassland. There was a car parked beside him. He was leaning on the car and was holding a bottle of beer in his hand. It was just about midday when Brady reached this place. "Too early for a man to be drunk. He might be in some kind of trouble." Brady moved closer to the man. He was crying and mumbling to himself. Brady stopped and enquired to the man if he was all right. The man slowly raised his head and looked at Brady's face. Then he lowered his head and continued to stare at the ground.

Brady waited for a few seconds; then he took out a packet of inexpensive cigarettes from his pocket. He searched for a lighter everywhere but, he could not find one. He looked at the person sitting on the grass and asked him if he had a lighter. The person took out the lighter from his pocket and handed it to Brady. Brady in return offered a cigarette to the man. The person took the proffered cigarette and kept it between his lips. Brady lighted the two cigarettes and handed the lighter back to the person. "You can keep it. I have another one somewhere". They both took a few puffs from their cigarettes in silence. Brady squatted on the grass beside the person. It is possible that, being in the company of a stranger may have calmed the person down. He introduced himself. "My name is Peter. I buried my best friend Joe this morning". Brady looked at him in sympathy. "I am sorry to hear that Peter." Brady sat quietly when he got no response. The afternoon rolled on and Peter had not said a word.

As the evening drew closer, Peter felt that he could now open up to this stranger who, took time to ensure that he will be all right. Peter explained to Brady that Joe's death was very sudden. It was like a lamp that blew out in a sudden gust of air. "I do know that everyone has to go someday, but some deaths and its nature cannot ever be justified or explained". Brady continued to sit in an attentive pose waiting for him to speak. He understood that this man needed someone to listen.

Peter continued to speak. "He was driving along the highway last week. Suddenly a large truck lost control and rammed into the back of his car. Joe who was driving slowly could not react appropriately and his car lost control and cartwheeled into the valley below. His body was mutilated beyond recognition. A life was lost for no reason."

Peter sat quietly for a little while. He then handed over a beer bottle to Brady from the pack that was on the ground beside him. Brady touched it to his forehead in salute and took a swig. They sat quietly for a few seconds. The gulping of the beer from the bottle was the only sound that emanated from them. A gentle breeze blew around them.

Peter further explained to Brady that Joe and his family were their neighbors and Joe had become his childhood friend. Their friendship had grown along with them and had increased with the passage of time. As they grew, their friendship had become an inseparable bond. But now he was separated from him by death.

Both their set of parents were long gone. Joe's lineage had died along with him.

They sat there for a very long time. Dusk drew closer and nightfall came. Crickets, badgers and bats came alive. The chirping, scurrying on the ground and flapping of the wings in the air from these creatures; drowned out the voice of the two humans, who were sitting there on the roadside on the outskirts of the woods.

The morning arrived bringing with it, cheerful sunshine and the chirping of the birds. Peter woke up to the sound of a baritone voice singing "I'll have a new life♫♫♫." He looked around in confusion. This was definitely his house and he was in his bedroom. But he was in street clothes with just the belt of his trousers loosened up and his shirt buttons were undone at the neck and the cuffs! He sat up bolt upright and a very nasty headache hit him viciously. He held his head in both his hands and lay back in bed. "Oh my God! How much did I drink last night?" He looked up to see Joe's face smiling at him from the picture frame on the mantlepiece of the fire place.

Slowly he remembered everything; including meeting this man he knew nothing about. He slowly got up from the bed and walked out into the living room. The voice was coming from the kitchen. He dragged his heavy legs and supported himself at the door. Brady turned around at the sound of the door and saw Peter. He wished him a very cheerful good morning.

He brought out two cups of coffee on a tray to the door. Peter let him pass and Brady brought the tray out to the breakfast table in the balcony. He dropped the awning on the balcony sufficiently enough; so that the direct rays of the sun will not hurt Peter's eyes and yet, they can get the required dose of sunshine. Peter continued to observe all of this quietly with interest. He was amused at how, Brady had made himself so comfortable in his house within the space of a morning. But he found it heart lifting to wake up to a cheerful voice for once. It had made a world of difference to his morning and he actually said it to Brady.

Peter took his usual seat and Brady sat across from him. Peter quietly remarked, "Brady, Joe used to sit there when he was visiting." Brady was scalded to hear this. He got up from the chair as if he was burnt, "Oh, sorry. I did not realise." Peter replied hurriedly with equal and terrible embarrassment, "Oh no, please sit down. I was just remarking at how effortlessly you were filling in the gap. It feels right". Brady again reminded Peter how sorry he was to hear about Joe's death and Peter's grief. Peter accepted his condolences gratefully. He knew that Brady was very sincere in his remarks. "Yes, he was a very dear friend and brother. He was full of humour and fun". Brady remained quiet.

There was an awkward silence. There was, only so much two virtual strangers can speak to each other. Yesterday was different! Peter did all the speaking. Now, they were both lost for words. Then Brady looked at Peter and thanked him for fixing him up with a bed last night. Peter waved it away

Peter wanted to know as to what was his next plan? Brady answered that he will look at the different rehabilitation programs that are offered to ex-prisoners. "Life as an ex-convict will not be easy. I don't have any family either." Peter enquired teasingly, "No girlfriend?" Brady informed Peter that he had a wife and an eleven year old son. He was bitter that she had divorced him and married someone else while he was in prison. Adding fuel to the fire, she applied for a barring order to prevent Brady from visiting his son. He could not see his son unless his son himself wished to make contact. "How can a person be so selfish?"

Peter softly remarked that relationships always changed during adversities. A woman may live all her life with the man she loved despite all his faults. And yet she may not be valued. If she complied, she was considered to be a door mat. But it actually takes strength of character to live such a life. It may be seen as weakness by others; but only the woman knows how much effort goes into living that kind of life. A woman who refuses to go through such a life is labelled a rebel. He asked Brady, "Do you know if she was happy with what you were doing? She may have taken your money for the sake of their son. When she saw a better chance of making a life without you, she took the opportunity". He added, "At least she made sure that she married a man who could provide for your child and considered the child as if he was his own. She also deserves a chance at her type of happiness".

Brady thought about what Peter said. "I suppose you are right." Peter just looked at him for a while. He then began to speak in a conciliatory tone: "I am not being the judge here. This is the way I am. I call a spade a 'spade'. If you can take gall, I am very happy for you to stay here until you want; even if it is for a short while. I have a garage. If you are interested, you can work there."

Brady laughed out loud and continued to laugh till his eyes watered. "You do know! It is car theft that landed me in jail." Peter smiled back at him. He however warned him that he was a law-abiding person and will definitely not pay under the table. However ironic it may sound; servicing the same cars for a living that he had stolen for fun, was a good offer.

"Look at it as your opportunity for redemption" Peter said to him. Brady was deep in thought. Peter was a sound person. He was kind and was giving him an opportunity to turn over a new leaf; a roof and a job. More valuable was his indirect offer of friendship.

After a while, Brady walked into the kitchen and rinsed his coffee mug. He came out of the kitchen and leaned over the door frame. He took a breath, looked at Peter directly in the eyes and remarked, "I better begin to earn my keep. I will clean the garage until you are ready and then you can show me around." After a small pause, he continued that he will try to live a straight life and if he could not cope with it, he will come outright and say it to

Peter.    Peter had already guessed Brady's nature and smiled at him. "It's a deal."

Another deal was occurring in another city in another country at the same time. The deal maker was Bob Walters.  He was being driven through the traffic of *Clapa Gopolini* by his chauffeur in an Aston Martin. He was spread on the rear passenger seat in a majestic style. Obviously! The car was his kingdom from which he conducted his business. The noise of the traffic was unbearable in the evening. The cars were honking at each other, the motor cyclists were revving their bikes to add to the chaos. The hawkers were crying out loud trying to sell their ware from the stalls on the roadside. Colorful awnings hung low from these stalls to shield the vendors and the customers from the piercing rays of the evening sun. These awnings when suspended at a low level; added to the traffic and the chaos but with the array of colors it gave the appearance of a beautiful rainbow. There was a lot of dust and the atmosphere was thick and foggy with the automobile fumes from the exhaust of the vehicles.

Despite all of these obstacles, Bob's car was sailing through; on the road effortlessly. The occupants of the air-conditioned car were oblivious to the noise and the pollution outside. Bob's assistant Monty was sitting in the front passenger seat. The built-in radio of the car was turned on. It was humming some classical music. When that came to an end, the anchor's voice reported the news that the secret service had revealed its largest ever siege of counterfeit money from Africa. The operation resulted in twenty-five arrests, seizure of three printing presses and hundreds of moulds. According to the news, the SS spokesperson was confident that they have reached the bottom of this network.

Bob sat up when he heard this piece of news. "I hope Marty is all right". Bob Walter is a heavily built tall man. He looked handsome in his tailored suit, tight haircut, clean shaven face and an expensive watch on his wrist. He was very smooth and suave. He had a series of legitimate businesses which acted as a front for his diamond smuggling, money laundering and counterfeit currency business. His net worth was over four hundred million Euros. He lived a careful life so that the public or the government were not aware of his shady deals. Yet he moved around in both circles; the upper world and the underworld alike with unrealistic ease. The mobile phone sitting on the dashboard chirped. Monty picked up the phone and looked at the caller identification on the display. He silently handed it over to Bob. Bob looked at the caller, accepted the call and said, "Hello Marty, I was just thinking about you--".

Marty spoke over Bob's acknowledgement and asked him if he had heard the news? Without giving Bob a chance to answer he said that he will speak about it later. "But at present, I need a favour from you". His partner Tommy, during the commotion; had fled with the diamonds which was their life savings. Marty further went on to explain that he had caught one of Tommy's loyal servants named Jack. He had confessed that Tommy had sailed towards *Clapa Gopolini* in his trawler 'Marissa'. "I will send you his details."

Bob reassured Marty, that if Tommy was anywhere near his city; he will catch him. Bob acknowledged to Marty that he knew that it was not a good time, but he needed counterfeit currency worth one million. "Can you organise it in your current situation?" Marty on the other end of the phone, shook his head in despair. He knew that Bob never did anything for free. "Well," he sighed. "One million is numerous times less than the actual worth of the diamonds" he consoled himself. He said, "Okay Bob, I will need time. Can you wait a few weeks?" Bob assured him to take as much time as he wanted. He will see Marty with the diamonds when he came to deliver the counterfeit currency. Marty signed off after saying goodbye. A few minutes later Bob's mobile phone pinged. He looked at the display and saw that there was a picture of Tommy with his trawler 'Marissa'. Bob handed over the phone to his assistant and asked him to have a good look at the picture. "We have a job to do boys. Have a good look at this bird that just migrated from Africa".

The driver kept his eyes on the road. He behaved as if he did not hear a thing. He was always supposed to act deaf around Bob's and Monty's conversation. He understood that there was a very valid reason for this. He would be the first target for Bob's enemies. They will torture him to pump information about Bob's whereabouts.

Bob did not employ girls not even as money pushers for this very reason. He thought that girls were weak and were only good enough to be draped around his arms looking beautiful. He did not have a permanent harem either. He just picked them up as he went along.

He could not bring himself to blame Bob for that. Seeing his expensive grooming and style was enough to get some girls eating out of his hands. One day hopefully; someone who is a very strong woman, will come along and get him to settle down. Despite his faults, he loved his boss. He was a very good employer to the employees that were loyal to him. His family was looked after very well because of the generous nature of his employer. His children had good education.

Bob's cronies went to the harbour in the evening after a few days. Sea gulls, crows, ducks, the Shearwaters and the Petrels were flying around very low over the water trying to settle for the night. The tide level was increasing slowly in response to the gravitational force of the moon. It was a brightly lit night. The moon was out in the height of its glory, hanging like a lantern over a clear sky. The smattering of clouds had a golden hue making it a very romantic evening for couples in love. The air was fresh and crisp.

The driver Paolo stayed in the car. Monty, Will, Anthony and Pedro got out of the car. They went over and checked out the boats that were anchored on the pier. Most of the fishermen and their boats were back from the ocean after their day of fishing. They will be here over the weekend and go back again on Monday. A few small boats with fishermen in wet suits were going out for night fishing. They will be back by dawn more likely with giant squids. The tourists were served fresh fish for lunch in all the restaurants around the coast. This was the morning's catch by the fishermen who left for the shallow waters at dawn.

Bob's men took their time going over the names of the various boats that were tied to the docks. Tommy's trawler 'Marissa' was nowhere to be seen. Paolo also looked around with his binoculars from the car. He answered the phone when it rang. Monty asked him if he could see the trawler even at a distance. Paolo answered in the negative.

Monty asked him to also check the boats that were out in the water. Especially the boats that were incoming. After a while they drove around the coast for a good length of time and for a good distance. Once they were satisfied that they had looked for the trawler high and low and couldn't find it; they decided to call Bob and report to him. They knew that he will not be happy, but it had to be done.

Bob answered the phone at the very first ring, "Yes". Monty hesitantly said to Bob that the 'Marissa' had not arrived yet.  Bob in actual fact was very cool. He asked them to keep an eye over the next few days. "The ladies of the various ports might be keeping him busy."

Monty asked if they could pump the harbour master for information? He did owe Bob a lot of favors. Bob was really angry when he heard this. He admonished Monty to shut up. Monty was really appreciating his foolishness by the end of this tirade.

Monty meekly terminated. "Sorry boss. Didn't think of that." Bob on the other hand, banged the phone down on its pedestal with a remark, "That is why I am the boss and not you". Monty was really upset. He called out to the boys in a subdued voice. "Let's do one more search boys, and then we can call it a night". The others murmured to each other. Will is the only person who answered, "Should we drive the coastal route into the next port?"

Monty explained to Will that to go and look for Tommy in another town was not an option. A person has a right to travel from one city to another. But when a criminal does the same thing frequently, his blood brothers will begin to take notice. "Bob will not be able to keep his facade of a gentleman for long, if that ever happened".

Will thanked God for being spared the diatribe from Monty. Will liked Monty very much. He was like a father figure to him. Moreover, he was gentle with everyone in the gang. Monty shielded all of them from Bob's anger. Will feared Bob and tried to stay out of his sight as much as possible. But sometimes he could not escape in spite of his best efforts. The whole day was then spent on making amendments. It did not happen often though. He did not have any other place to go. This gang was the only place he knew since he was a child.

## Chapter 3: October 29th 14:30

The district court house was very busy and full of people. The lawyers were going in and coming out of the courts irregularly but frequently. There was an air of importance in their faces. The police vehicles drew up into the parking and brought in suspects to be remanded to jail or for bail hearings. They all walked in to different court rooms with their prisoners. Some prisoners came very jubilant and happy and some came out very withdrawn out of the court room after the hearing.

Another police vehicle drew up into the parking lot of the courthouse. Police officer Duke got out of the passenger seat of the car. He opened the passenger door at the back. Duke helped Jason to get out of the car. He was handcuffed. Today was the day of the parole hearing that Jason had been waiting for impatiently. Police officer Mike who was driving the car got out and locked the car with his keys. He played with the bunch of keys for a little while. Then he clipped the bunch on to his holster belt. Jason walked into the court house of his own accord with high expectations. He was very anxious. His parole request had been denied many times already. He had served ten years now. "Surely the judges should be satisfied?"

At 1700 hours, Jason and the two officers walked out of the court house. Jason's face was like thunder. He was very furious. His parole was denied yet again. They stood on the portico of the courthouse. There were many other people standing there to protect their eyes from the setting rays of the evening sun. Mike who has the phone in his hand was speaking to the prison warden Stone who was on the phone on the other end. Duke and Jason walked ahead of Mike because he had slowed down to dial the mobile phone. "Hello Mike from the court house. We are on our way to the prison with Jason". Stone asked about the outcome of the hearing. "What's the story?" Mike replied, "The judge was not in favour."

Stone was speaking on the other end and it was a very long conversation. Mike transferred the phone to his left hand and unclipped the bunch of keys with his right hand. The bunch slipped and fell to the floor. Mike quickly bent over to pick up the keys. A person moved in between Mike and Jason and slipped a rolled-up piece of paper into Jason's handcuffed palm. Jason quickly folded his hand. Mike picked up the key and looked up while concentrating on the conversation on the other end. Someone was crossing the car park in wide strides just in front of him. There was nothing out of the ordinary. The three of them continued to walk to the parking lot.

Mike continued his conversation with Stone, "Yeah, I know. It is a pity. He is a model prisoner. But I don't blame the tax payers. They want to keep him behind the bars. They are just exacting their due. The law is there for a reason!"

Stone agreed with Mike but in his own heart, he felt very sorry for Jason. There were more serious kinds of financial wrongs happening all over the world. Corruption, millions of Euros ending up in the Swiss Bank with the account holder not even alive to claim it. He asked Mike to keep the report on his table ready to be signed off in the morning. He then discontinued the conversation.

Jason and Duke were already waiting near the car. Mike hastened to open the car door. Duke is annoyed and distracted because Mike was slow in unlocking the car. He got Jason to sit inside and closed the car door. Jason quickly moved his leg closer to the door. His thick shoe lace got stuck between the door and the legroom. But Mike did not check if the door was properly locked or not. He sat down in the passenger seat. They were late already!

Jason and the police officers were now driving through the courthouse gates and on to the main street. In a few minutes, the car was speeding along the coastal road. The police radio was turned on in the car. They can hear instructions from the headquarters being relayed to the various patrol units. Duke is snoozing in the passenger seat in the front. Mike looked at him and smiled to himself, "Looks like Duke had spent a very busy night with his wife". Jason carefully unrolled the tiny piece of paper and felt for the object that was kept inside. It was a key. He wriggled his wrists carefully and after several attempts released the hand cuff gently. He stayed in that position for a good while. Blood circulated more freely through his veins. He looked at Duke and was relieved to see that he continued to snooze.

Mike's attention was focused at the traffic on the road. Jason crawled his hand forward slowly millimeter by millimeter and tried to open the passenger door. It was heavy and difficult to open without attracting the attention of the two policemen. He painstakingly repeated the hand movement in the opposite direction and repositioned his hand at his back. He looked at Duke again and notices that he is still asleep.

The drive will be a good seventy minutes. Jason continued to keep watch for a suitable place to execute his escape. It had to be near the water. Once the car turns into the wood land for a twenty kilometre stretch, his chances of success will be narrowed. He can now see the ocean in the far distance. Duke continued to drive unaware of what Jason was doing at the back.

Fifty minutes left! Jason began to become anxious. The scenery on the road side is lush green in a backdrop of light blue water. The green bushes have large flowers with vibrant colors; it looks like a colorful hue as the car speeds by. Jason is not cognisant of any of these. His eyes are calculating the level of the water and its distance from the road.

Eventually, the water appeared closer and the distance between the road and the water became about three hundred meters. Thirty minutes left to reach the prison! He has to take his chances now. It is a gamble worth playing. If he manages to escape; it will be brilliant. If not, then he will be the prison warden's special guest for the remainder of his stay! "Don't forget the extended punishment you will receive for trying to make them look like fools" he admonished himself mentally. A shiver ran through Jason's spine at the thought. The water was at two hundred meters distance now.

Mike suddenly turned a sharp corner at high speed. The car lurched from side to side. Jason, in the wink of an eye undid his seat belt. He leaned heavily on the door which opened because of his exertion and also because it was not locked properly. The door was just wedged and remained unlocked because of the shoe lace. He pushed with all his strength to open the car door and jumped out. He broke his fall by rolling on the ground, somersaulting as he fell. Mike was taken by surprise and the car skidded out of control. The screeching of the tyres as Mike tried to regain control was like someone rubbing a barbed wire through a person's ears!

Duke woke up with a start at the commotion! All of this had occurred in a split second. He was in shock and was trying to comprehend the scene that was unfolding before him. As soon as Mike slowed the car, he jumped out and chased Jason. He pulled out his revolver and attempted to shoot him. It was a mammoth effort for Jason to jump out of a speeding car and escape unharmed.

Dodging the volley of bullets was another skilled manoeuvre! The adrenaline in his body had urged him to the water's edge and now the Adrenaline rush was at its peak. He lunged into the water with all his might. For his height, he was now knee deep in water. He kept his head low which hindered Duke's efforts to get a clear shot at Jason. The sea wall and the reeds shielded him from Duke's sight and bullet. Mike had stopped the car by now;

he alerted the local police station and then the prison. His call for immediate back up was heard and responded to.

He then joined Duke who was running to the water's edge, but he could not see Jason. Mike swore at Jason in despair. He looked helplessly at Duke. Jason meanwhile had dived deep under the water; well below the surface and was swimming out to the open sea. He was cold and shivering but the adrenaline and the thought of the consequences if caught, kept him going.

Slowly his body adjusted to the temperature of the water. He swam up to the surface frequently to get some air. He swam for a long time; only surfacing when absolutely necessary. He could now see the hull of a vessel in the far distance. He swam towards it as if drawn by a beacon of hope. He still had a good bit to go.

After a long time, Jason latched on to the vessel and looked back.

The coastal area was in the far distance and flooded with blue lights and the sound of police siren pierced the night air. Back up had arrived at the scene. They were there in their full strength. Because of the darkness, the visibility level was low; the helicopters could not spot him as he had been deep under the ocean for a good while. Jason was grateful for the small mercies.

Next day, the policemen were sitting in the conference room of the local police station. The room was full. It was five o clock in the morning. The police chief Aaric walked in and took the podium. He is all business. He coughed discretely to bring his team to immediate order and silence. The Chief of Police thanked them for assembling so early in the morning. People already had heard about Jason's escapade, but they now wanted to hear the juicy bits. They were really glad; even if it meant more work for them all. They were true professionals and they will try their level best to bring him back!

But the correctional officers had got their comeuppance. They always acted very high and mighty when they came together for the combined study days for the department of law and enforcement. "They were a snooty lot and they got their just dessert" some of them thought in their heads. The light in the room dimmed immediately and the projector screen on the wall illuminated with Jason's photo on it.

Chief Aaric read out the case history of Jason from the file that was kept in front of him. Jason was convicted for an imprisonment of fifteen years with the possibility of Parole. He had served ten years of his sentence already. He was denied Parole for the remaining five last evening. He escaped from the car, when he was being escorted back from the court house. The photos of the four ex-convicts who were his friends and were now serving parole; was also projected on the screen.

Chief Aaric discussed them individually. When he came to Lucas he remarked, "He is the least favoured person in this group. He will be probably the first one to break; if they even remotely knew anything. His loyalty is towards himself. He is in the group only by virtue of being David's twin brother." Chief Aaric drew a breath. This speech summed up all the details that the police had about these people on their records.

The lights came back on in the conference room. Everyone blinked at the sudden change in the level of the illumination. Chief Aaric took a sip of water from the glass that was kept on the podium. He looked at it with distaste. It was lukewarm! He would have preferred a cup of coffee mixed with some brandy. He has been up all-night listening to the rant from Warden Stone. He had not even been able to use the toilet.

The prison warden, Stone was his friend and Aaric owed him his life. Stone had taken a bullet for him when they were on the beat together. That was a life time ago! Stone was now out for Jason's blood. Aaric jolted back from his reverie. He continued "the files that are kept on the tables in front of you contain all of these details and their addresses. Each team has been allocated with their respective assignment. Everyone match the time on your watches. Today is the 29th of October and time is 5:30 am. Now, get to work. I need him back by six this evening. I have made dinner arrangements for him with the prison warden for tonight. Is that understood?" They all answered with one voice, "Yes sir". Everyone got up immediately and left the room to go about their tasks. There was an air of excitement; as if they were going to hunt animals.

## Chapter 4: October 29th 05:30

When chief Aaric was giving instructions to his men; Jason was hiding in the lower level stow away compartment of the 'Mocking Bird'. He went into the vessel's galley in the middle of the night and stole some meat, bread and beer. He ate to his heart's content and laid his head on a sack. He could feel round structured soft things in the sack. Probably the sack was filled with potatoes by the feel of it. He drifted in and out of sleep.

All night he was disturbed by sound of the creaking noise of the beer barrels rubbing against each other and the hull of the vessel. He could hear the storm raging outside and the boat rocking wildly in the storm. For a minute, he was afraid. "Well," he thought that it was a sea faring vessel and should remain stable. "No one can stop destiny. If I am meant to die, then so be it." He did not have the luxury to look around and be discovered. He was not in international waters when he had boarded the vessel, so he was worried. He would have been handed very quickly over to the port authorities of the city that he had escaped from if caught!

It was good that he did not suffer from motion sickness or he would have puked everywhere. However, the deeper you are in the belly of the ship, the less motion sickness a person will feel. Despite all of this; if he did puke, the smell of vomit would have been a perfect give away to the cook who came to the store room in the morning. He had come down to collect food stores. Jason who had heard the footsteps shuffle slowly down the ladder; moved deep into the bowel of the boat. He had come in contact with a bag of flour in his desperate attempt to hide.

The flour dust compelled him to sneeze. He held his breath in spite of that and somehow was able to distract himself. He breathed out with relief when the cook eventually left. He spent the whole day in the bottom of the vessel. Time stretched ahead of him. He was not a person to sit quietly if he could afford to. He spent his time alternating between snoozing and exercising; combined with successful attempts at hiding.

Eventually, the 'Mocking Bird' docked in the harbour. It was late evening. The setting sun was at the level of the water in the horizon. One last attempt to spread the orange glow before the world plunged into darkness. Jason could see all of this from the porthole; yet, he stayed put for a long time. He had felt plenty of movements in the ship. People were beginning to get off the vessel. Goods were being off-loaded to the shore.

The captain of the vessel was bargaining with the harbour master to let him unload some minor contraband stuff. It seemed that the harbour master had denied his request and left. He deduced this because a singular voice was heard complaining for a long time. He assumed this to be the voice of the captain. The rant ended eventually. The noises ceased gradually and could be heard fading in the distance after a long time had passed. He gathered from the conversation of the crew that they were going to spend the night on the shore

Jason relaxed but he did not move from his position. Now was the time to be extremely careful. If there was even one person remaining in the ship, his movements will alert them to his presence. He was nearly there, and he did not want to be caught at home stretch. He stayed like that for a long time.

Once he heard no more noises except the soft lapping of the water against the boat, he got out from his hiding place. He walked around the vessel; inspecting and staking the place out. He found some clothes that were hanging in one of the berths. They just about fitted him. He will have to manage with those for a while.

He saw that the fire in the oven in the galley was turned down but not extinguished totally. There was a pot of something on a slow boil. It looked like beef stew. He had seen the cook cut a piece of meat from the carcass hanging in the hull. It has been cooking for the whole day then! The meat will be nice and tender. He burnt his prison clothes in the embers of the oven fire. He helped himself to some of the hot stew from the pot, dipped his finger in the bowl and licked the hot stew from his finger. "Yum" it has been a while since he had tasted anything so delicious. The prison food lacked imagination. "Well, they were preparing food for the scum of society as far as they were concerned". He thought to himself.

At last he ventured to the deck. He looked around. He had no clue as to where he was and what city. He decided to spend the night in the boat. He will wake up and leave the vessel at dawn. He slept very well that night in the confidence that the vessel was empty.

Staying awake the previous night now enveloped him into a dreamless sleep. Several hours later, he woke up with a start. He stayed awake but did not move. He listened for noises. There was none. He looked outside, through the porthole. It was dark outside. He slowly ventured from his hiding place. He sneaked up to the bridge and checked the time on the clock. It was nearly evening the next day the 31st of October. He admonished himself with lenience. "Tiredness was no excuse. What if you had been caught?" He smiled to himself.

He was glad that so far he was safe. He got up, took a big stretch and used the boat head to relieve himself. He ventured out to the deck again. Because of the weather, the pier was empty. Rain was lashing heavily. He has to leave! The weather is no excuse! He did not know for how long they were docked or when the crew will make an appearance. He could not stay in this vessel forever. He needed to hide somewhere on land safely. He skipped on to another vessel and then on to another vessel coming closer and closer to the pier. Soon very soon, he will be on dry land. "Terra firma' here I come."

The 'Marissa' was docked in the pier. Tommy and his bodyguard, Augustine were sitting on the roof of the cabin. They were shielded from the rain by the Bimini top. Both of them were drinking alcohol and enjoying their time. It was a warm evening, despite the rain. Tommy was the partner who had cheated Marty of his diamonds and had escaped. These were the people Bob's gang was looking for. Tommy is seated facing the sea front and Augustine was facing the harbour. Tommy commented that by now their partner Jack would have been caught by Marty and his gang. Augustine respectfully told his boss, "Hope that is not the case." Marty shook his head emphatically. He knew that his belief was correct. "Jack was not a person who could withstand torture. He will have divulged their destination by now," he concluded.

After some time of contemplation, Tommy continued, "We have been docked here for three days now. We have had a run of good weather and a good time during this journey. Now we should move on". Tommy further asked Augustine if their skipper Mathias who had gone out to shop; will have the common sense to purchase enough material for the next leg of their journey. Augustine laughed at his boss "Do you not know that Mathias by nature is a hoarder?" What they had brought from Africa will be even now enough to last them for another two weeks! Tommy is annoyed by his crony's complacence. He does not really understand how important it is to stock up when a person was traveling via the ocean. "There is no greater irony than dying of thirst when surrounded by miles of water!"

The trawler experienced a lurching movement suddenly. Tommy and Augustine looked at each other. Augustine calmly replied that it might be Mathias sneaking back on them. "Think of the devil. Yo hoo Mathias, you are back already? Hey Mathia—s"

There was no answer. Augustine looked at Tommy; he signalled to him to go down and check. Augustine got up from his chair and looked around. He slowly and quietly descended the staircase into the next level. Jason held his breath when he heard Augustine call out Mathias' name. It was him jumping on board the 'Marissa' that had caused the lurch. He had to think fast! If he didn't hide, he will be caught very soon. He looked around desperately. He sank further into the wall of the cruiser. His hip struck against something hard. He looked back; it was a live well! It was right behind him full of shark bait and a few sea gulls were flying around it.

He moved the lid of the live well and moved a few steps away. He gently placed the lid upside down, haphazardly. He then got a shark bait, a heavy fish from the live well and slid it on the floor. Then he concealed himself very carefully behind the hatch. The cacophony of the sea gulls increased manyfold; on free access to the live well. They all swooped in to get hold of the fish simultaneously. Some of the sea gulls dived in to the live well again to catch more fish. The trawler lurched further combined with the wind, the heavy rain and the waves that were crashing madly.

Augustine was very annoyed at Mathias for playing around. He walked down the stairs in a hurry. When he saw the lid of the live well on the floor and the sea gulls swooping for the fish; he relaxed completely. "How did the sea gulls manage to do this?" He asked himself. "Mathias is a careful man but sometimes he can be very stupid! This definitely looks like his carelessness". He came down, shooed away the birds and replaced the lid back on top of the live well. As an extra measure, he took a fishing net that was lying nearby and covered the top of the live well loosely. He then in his haste to get away from the elements, walked back up to the cabin top. He was soaking wet by then!

Tommy looked up in enquiry. Augustine smiled broadly. "Just the sea gulls looking for their dinner." Tommy smiled. Augustine sat down and picked up his glass. Jason heard this conversation and heaved a sigh of relief. He did not want to attract further attention. He decided not to move from there for some time. He inched his way down into the hull and sat huddled in a corner. He was shivering with anxiety. He could not afford to get caught after having come this far. He shrank into himself further. He then closed his eyes. Slowly he relaxed, but he did not move.

Meanwhile Tommy and Augustine continued to enjoy their evening. Augustine lifted up his glass to empty the last drop when a white coloured car appeared in his line of vision. Another car joined to make a convoy. He held the glass in midair and continued to carefully watch the cars. Tommy who sensed a change in Augustine's behaviour looked up. He did not understand why Augustine was behaving like this; so, he turned around to see what he was looking at.

He also noticed the car driving down the harbour road and looked back at his deputy; who asked Tommy, "Friend or foe?" Tommy's golden policy was to treat anyone as a foe until he knew exactly who they were. The cars halted at a distance. A man got out of the car and looked around at the vessels moored on the pier. He saw 'Marissa' at the distance. He looked back to the car and raised his thumb in confirmation. Both the car doors opened in response to the thumbs up immediately. People got out of the car with a sense of purpose. The passenger from the front seat of the car got out and opened the rear passenger door.

Bob got out of the car and looked around with great pomp. He straightened his suit and walked forward. His men followed him. Tommy and Augustine were standing up by now. Tommy pulled his gun out of his holster. "Definitely a foe," he answered to Augustine's earlier question. Bob saw the gun in Tommy's hand, but he did not pay heed. He walked into the trawler with his cronies. He walked up to the cabin top. He raised up his left hand and smiled, "Welcome to my city, my kingdom!" Tommy stared at him and raised the gun further. Bob who had his hands in his suit pocket now acknowledged the raised gun. He pointed out that it was not a good idea. The tension was high in the air. Tommy wanted to know what Bob wanted. Bob laughed, "You very well know what I want. A little bird gave away your secret."

Tommy looked anxiously at Augustine. The non-verbal language was meant to convey that the secret was out. It cannot be hidden anymore. He looked at Bob and lowered his gun. Tommy asked Bob, "Okay, what is the deal?" Bob looked at his assistant Monty and smiled. Monty smiled back at his boss. Bob now turned back to look at Tommy and smiled even more widely. "Tommy, since you cheated your partner Marty out of the diamonds, you are not in a position to negotiate. You do not deserve any share in the diamonds." Tommy is really flabbergasted. He risked his life to get the diamond from his partner. He had travelled a long and arduous sea route in a conventional small trawler to get here and now Bob walked in regally as if he had the sole right to the stash of diamonds. But he had no choice. He was sure that Bob had come prepared

Marty must have engaged him for a reasonable portion of the diamond. He was busy thinking on those lines and deciding his next move. While Augustine on the other hand, attempted to pull out his gun which was tucked in his trouser at the back. Bob who had already anticipated this move; pulled out his hand from his coat pocket. The hand was already holding a pistol! He shot first at Augustine and then aimed for Tommy. Both of them dropped dead on the floor in seconds. Bob did not even look at them. He blew at the barrel of his gun as if blowing off the smoke. "No deal" He laughed. He kept the gun back in his pocket. He walked over Tommy and Augustine's dead body and reached Monty. He looked at Monty. "Go find the diamonds."

Monty walked down to the lower deck. He did not even know where to begin! He checked the saloon and then walked into the berths. He looked around for a suitable hiding place. He had no clue as to where Tommy may have hidden the diamonds. He looked at the headboard of the bed and under the chairs. He did not even have an idea of how much diamond was there and in what receptacle? Criminals have a bond of trust towards each other; but this trust does not extend to the intricate finer details. Marty could have easily lied about the quantity of the diamond. Or Tommy may have removed some of them or it may not be here at all. Who knows?

He noticed that a few briefcases were stowed away in the lockers under the berths. Monty opened one case after next and he eventually found the diamonds in a light coffee colored briefcase. It had a 'green eyed monster' sticker stuck on the top. Monty was dumb struck. The brilliance of the diamonds in the small enclosed space, was amazing. The sun's rays entering from the porthole made the diamonds glimmer. To Monty it appeared as if the diamonds were winking at him. He was open mouthed with wonder! He looked away very quickly. The brilliance was blinding his eyes. He did not even touch the diamonds. He knew the consequences of greed.

He was not beyond temptation, but his loyalty exceeded his greed. He closed the briefcase and walked out of the cabin. He came to the upper deck and handed the case over to Bob. Bob took the briefcase and instructed Monty and the men to tidy up the trawler. Monty spoke to the men and walked out with Bob. They both walked to the cars and sat inside.

Jason opened his eyes in fright when the trawler lurched as Bob and his men boarded the 'Marissa'. Different types of footsteps could be heard climbing aboard. This definitely was not the third thug called Mathias. These were too many footsteps to be made by one person. He stayed quietly for a while trying to understand what was happening. Then he slowly crawled on his hands and knees to where he could hear the conversation properly. He heard the interaction between Tommy and Bob. He could see the nervous energy flowing in both the men.

The air of tension was palpable. He had seen enough murderers in the last ten years to recognise one. "Fantastic" he thought, "out of the fire and into the frying pan!" He followed Monty to the berths and had seen the diamonds. When Monty left to go up to the upper deck with the diamonds, Jason entered the berths and looked around. He had to think and work fast. He found some good quality clothes, a few debit cards, passport and some money. He stuffed everything into his pocket. He felt the vessel lurch again; so, he stayed motionless for a few minutes.

Now he heard more cheerful voices coming from the upper deck. "So, the man with the whip has left. His cronies are tying up the loose ends." Jason's head was screaming for him to get out of the trawler. He quickly and deftly climbed out of the trawler on to the dock. He walked towards the car park. He had his eyes focussed on Bob and Monty. He was careful so that his presence will not be detected. The heavy rain was in his favour. Bob and Monty reached their car. The driver opened the car door for them. Monty assisted Bob into the car as usual. He then opened the front door and sat down in the passenger seat. The driver turned the ignition on and waited.

After a while Bob's men also returned to the cars and they drove away together. When they reached the harbour gates, they saw a homeless man who sits down at the gates to beg. He followed the convoy with his eyes for a distance. He saw that the boot of the car was slightly open and bobbing up and down slowly. He just sat there and minded his own business. "Better turn a blind eye." He had seen a lot worse. Men were shot for the most stupid reasons. Prostitutes were knifed to death after their service. Young women were raped so they will not be a witness. Children were trafficked for money. The people who were involved in these crimes knew that he saw everything; but they also knew that he will not open his mouth. He valued his life and was only worried about his stomach. The rest of the world could go up in ashes and he couldn't care less! Another man who walked into the harbour also turned around to look at the convoy as well. He also saw what the homeless man had seen. He just shrugged his shoulders and kept walking.

The man who had observed the car in the harbour, now entered the 'Marissa'. He called out as he jumped on board, "Ahoy, I am back." No response! He found it strange that Augustine was not answering him. He went up to the lower deck and looked up. He saw that Tommy and Augustine were lying on the floor with blood all around them. He quickly ducked under the canopy and pulled out his gun. He stayed quiet for a while and tuned his ears to the silence. He could not hear any noise. Slowly he lifted his head up above the canopy carefully and looked around. He did not see or hear anyone. He rushed forward to his friends and found that they were both dead. He looked around for clues. He remembered the cars driving by. He went down to the berths and checked the cases. The briefcase with the 'green eyed monster' sticker was missing. "So, whoever had come, knew about the diamonds!" he thought to himself. They killed his friends and took the briefcase.

Mathias went back to the upper deck. He sat beside his friends for a while and drank the alcohol that was left in the bottle. When he poured out the last shot, he toasted them both. He drained the glass and threw it viciously on the deck. The glass shattered into pieces. He sat like that for a long time. Then he went out of the trawler down to the pier. He chose two large boulders and hauled it into the vessel. He then set sail at around midnight. He sang a very melancholic song to combat his loneliness. He remembered his friends and the good times they had shared together as a group. The whole activity showed the love he had for his friends. He was undertaking a funeral procession for them. It was their last journey and he wanted it to be a nice procession for them.

He reached the international waters without any problem. He turned off the engine. The weather was dry, crisp and the clean ocean air raced through his lush black hair like wind passing between the grasslands. He went up to the upper deck with a few ruck sacks. He looked at his friends for a few more minutes again. He will never see them after this. He packed them individually into the rucksacks. He dragged the bodies to the edge one by one with difficulty. He said a prayer for them both and then handed them reverently over into the loving arms of the ocean. The bodies of his friends slowly descended down to the bottom of the sea. They now became the dinner for the sharks that they had once dined on! Mathias set sail towards the horizon; the rising sun welcomed him with both arms.

From the harbour, Bob's car travelled through the coastal road. Up and down past the winding sand dunes. The men were chatting away. They were on a high after their successful venture. The decorum was only maintained because of Bob's presence in the car. The phone rang and Monty answered it. "Hello?" He listened to the caller on the other end. His demeanour was suddenly very respectful. "Oh yes sir, 'big daddy' is here. I will hand the phone to him now" he answered. He looked at Bob, "Your uncle sir".

Bob took the phone from Monty and spoke into the phone. "Hello uncle, this is Bob." How are you? ------ Oh no, Monty will bring the gold biscuits to you tomorrow, we had another assignment today" He listened to the conversation from the other end for a while, "Okay uncle, good night. I will speak to you tomorrow". He handed the phone back over to Monty. They drove for a good distance. It was late evening by the time Bob and his men reached the villa. The rain was still lashing, and the darkness had increased manyfold. The driver of the first car blared the horn at the gates. The security guard came running. The driver of the first car got out. He is very annoyed now!

He had to get out in the rain because of this man's laziness! He walked quickly to the gate and admonished the security. "What's the problem man? Why are you not opening the gate? You know that, 'big daddy' will become angry". Security replied apologetically "Sorry Antonio, I tried the remote, but it is not opening." Together they looked at the gate. Something was wedged under one of the gates. The driver attempted to remove it, but he was not able to do so. He went to the second car and Monty slid the windscreen down. "What is the problem?" he asked the driver. The driver looked at Bob and reported that the gate was stuck. Monty opened the door of the car and got out. "I will get the tools from the boot."

Monty went to the back of the car and opened the boot. He was surprised that the boot was already open. He could not remember leaving it open! He did not say anything to anyone but looked around carefully. There was no one there. He shrugged his shoulders, got the tools from the boot and handed it to the driver.

He had seen a cuff link from a coat lying on the floor of the boot, but he threw it away. He did not pay much heed. It could be his own cuff link for all he knew! He had one that looked something like it. Monty went with the driver to the gate to observe the proceedings. He will be an extra pair of hands if required. The driver, with the help of Monty and after a few attempts removed the obstacle. The gate which was whirring away motionlessly now slid open without any effort. Both the cars drove in and Bob got out and went into the house.

A pair of eyes was observing everything from behind a tree. Jason who had travelled in the boot had got out when everyone's attention was at the gate. He continued to watch the gate and the house for some time. He would not have been able to get out of the house easily if the gate was not stuck and they had driven in. The house was alive and active until early morning. After a while of watching and waiting, he went away from there.

## CHAPTER 5: OCTOBER 31st 18:00

The market place was full of people. The various stalls were holding a variety of colorful goods. The mobile carts carried different seasonal items on them for sale. Today was the night of the Halloween. The streets were very crowded. Day light was slowly giving in to the man-made electrical lights, bonfires and the lights from firecrackers. The people were all in good spirits. Young couple are out and about holding hands and looking at the goods in the stalls.

A vendor was selling color powders on an open cart. A person grabbed a handful of purple color and rubbed it thickly across his face. The vendor looked up in alarm! He was terrified that he was being robbed. But the person kept a fifty Euro note on the cart. The vendor looked down at the note. When he saw the money, he looked up happily. The person was not there anymore. 'Well,' he shrugged his shoulder. There was more value in that one note when compared to his anticipated earnings for the entire evening.

He was about to leave, when a couple walked up to him and bought some colors from him. They paid with small change and then rubbed color on each other's face with laughter and fun. The vendor took part in their happiness and went off home rolling his cart. He was skipping with joy as well. Now he can enjoy the holiday with his family.

The man with the purple face walked up to a nearby hotel. The foyer is very busy. He can see many families sitting around and having a good time. Looked like the whole world was here for the big day. Obviously not all of them came with the aim of visiting this sleepy little coastal town; the name of which now he learned was *Clapa Gopolini.* The hospitality industry in the city was probably overbooked. The receptionist was busy at the desk. She is laughing and smiling with the customers. The receptionist looked up to see a man with his face totally covered in color. The hotel was providing drinks on the house for the day. She had helped herself to more than what she could tolerate. She looked at Jason and laughed out loud. Jason smiled at her. He knew that he looked like a comedian. Seeing his smile, she laughed even louder and continued till her belly ached. "Oh, you look so cute. What can I do for you?" She laughingly asked Jason. He brought out his best and charming smile and asked for a single room. The receptionist's interest is now perked up.

She allocated him a double room for the price of a single suite. Jason gave Tommy's passport on her request for identification. She took the passport from him and glanced at it cursorily. She took a photocopy of the passport and then returned the original passport to Jason. She then opened the cabinet behind her to file the printed copy. She looked back towards the front of the house as she heard some commotion. Unknown to her, the passport copy fell on the floor and slid under the cabinet. The receptionist closed the drawer under the assumption that the passport copy was filed. She handed over the room key to Jason with a charming smile. "Enjoy your stay sir. Please let me know if you need anything during the night. I am here on duty." No one can under estimate Jason. He can charm anyone's socks off. He thanked her with a beautiful smile and walked to the staircase. He was relieved that he got a safe place to stay safe for the night.

He went to the second floor and opened the room allocated to him. He walked in and locked the door from the inside. He fell onto the bed. He is safe at last. He can relax. All the noise from the streets outside is like music to his ears which sang a lullaby just for him. The memory of the movement of the boat on the ocean matched the street noise and rocked him softly to sleep. The gentle cold breeze made him hug the blanket closely to himself. He slept like a baby after so many years.

Jason woke up very early in the morning. It was a habit from the prison. He sat up and stretched in the soft luxurious bed. He felt very fresh. The receptionist was very generous to him. He was worried for a minute about her intentions. She was harmless in the end. He may not have heard her even if she did come knocking. His stomach grumbled loudly. He was suddenly very hungry. He had not eaten anything since last night. He walked into the shower and luxuriated in the warm water and the fragrant shower gel. He walked out of the bathroom and got ready. "Breakfast first and then some shopping for disguise" he said to himself. He hung the hat low on his forehead. He took a leisurely walk down the stairs and was half way down when, he saw a policeman asking questions to someone at the door of a room on the first floor. He had a photograph in his hand.

Jason began to perspire profusely. He looked down to the other end of the corridor. He saw two policemen bringing a man out from one of the rooms. At least this one was not for him, "Thank God!" Jason decided to go back to his room. Fortunately, he looked back before going back up the stairs. A policeman was standing at the top of the landing. Jason turned slowly around and casually walked down. He saw a seating area on the spacious landing. He walked over to the seating area and sat down beside a man who was reading a magazine. He acknowledged the man seated on the chair, and picked up a newspaper. He covered his face in the pretext of reading it. Jason's hands were really trembling with fear.

A policeman walked by very slowly. He was looking at the two men intently. His heart lurched into his mouth. The policeman left after a few minutes. It felt like years to Jason. In a little while, he heard the sound of the sirens fading away in the distance. "Pooh, that was close!" Jason put the newspaper down slowly. "No, today it has to be room service. The rest can wait for another day. It's too early to go out," he decided. He walked back into his room and locked it behind him. He checked it at least thrice and then he sat down for a little while on the bed.

He was breathing heavily. To him, it felt as if a thousand demons had chased him. Yes, the police force was his current nemesis. He reflected on his situation. He cannot continue to live like this; looking over his shoulders all the time. He had to do something about it. "Well, I will order room service first and then make a decision." He picked up the phone and ordered what he wanted. His appetite was gone but he had to keep his energy level up. He then sat down on the bed and watched the news on the television.

It was two days; before Jason regained the courage to come out of the hotel building. His wide brimmed hat was hanging low over his eyes. He looked around carefully. The hotel was beside a major road of a small town. The road was flanked with a generous footpath on either side. There was a supermarket on one side of the road and a unisex saloon. A bank of international repute was on that side as well. "This is the bank" he thought to himself, "I saw from my room window yesterday". There was a coffee shop beside it and a cloth merchant made up the row of establishments on that side. Beside the hotel was a solicitor's office, a real estate agent and a police station on this side of the road. All the basic amenities required to live in a small coastal town was here on this one street. The only thing missing was a hospital and a funeral home. It could be anywhere in the village. Not that he needs either. A cute little town with a cute little name!

The color and crowd from Halloween was long gone. Christmas decorations were slowly being put up in the shops. He went into the supermarket and bought some grooming items, a few fruits, drinks, bars of chocolate, a pair of sunglasses and a make-up kit. He also bought stationary; an easel, drawing papers, pencil, sharpener, eraser, assortment of brushes and oil paint. He walked around the town and got to know the places. He had to present a facade to the curious people that he will possibly meet. This sleepy seaside town was very beautiful. The people were very kind. Beautiful beaches made up the coastline and the sun shined down benevolently. The rambling hills on the far side bordered a fertile valley in between. The farms and the grazing land were large in size and lush green. A beautiful place to live. There were a number of villas on the coastal road in the far distance.

After checking out the village; Jason went back to his room and neatly kept his purchases away. This was another habit from the prison. There were raids every week in their cells. The inmates themselves were responsible for cleaning their own living accommodation. If it was not clean enough, they were given corridor duty for a full month. That meant that they had to clean the corridor of the entire building by themselves along with their other assigned tasks. Moreover, they were jeered and ridiculed by the other inmates.

He first altered his appearance. His short hair was growing long now. After such a long time of keeping the hair cropped short, he felt it very awkward to feel his own hair. It lay heavy on his head. He was due for a haircut in the prison; but he got out before that. He decided to let his hair grow. He decided to bleach his moustache, eyebrow and hair. His dark brown hair changed into a bleached blonde. The overnight stubble cast a shadow on his face. He had not shaved since the day he had escaped. He was going to use an artificial beard for the time being. He thought that it will be better for the original one to grow long. He just had to be careful that all of his original beard was covered properly under the false one. It will be a costly mistake if he did not cover his beard properly. He groomed himself for a good while and inspected himself in the mirror critically. "Not bad" he thought to himself. He then washed one of the apples he had purchased and bit into it. He turned on the radio. Soft melodious song was playing in the background. He felt relaxed with the music. He set the paper on the easel and began to coat the paper with a base layer of paint. He drew a few long horizontal strokes and a few vertical smooth lines. Jason kept the brush down, when the music coming from the radio ended. The outline of the coastal town had begun to appear in Jason's canvas. It was an amateur effort, but it was just a front. He made a coffee on the percolator provided in the room and went to the window. He kept the coffee on the window sill and looked out. People were going about their business. He went back to his painting after a while. He thought about his friends. "What were they all doing? Were they able to adjust living in the society of the self-proclaimed good people?"

Peter and Brady were working in the garage together. The cars were all parked neatly in order. Peter was changing the headlights of a car while Brady was changing the tyre. They were very busy. A few cars had been left over the weekend. They heard the sound of a car driving up the road and looked up. A patrol car pulled up at the kerb. The two policemen got out and stood near the car. Peter and Brady looked at each other. Suddenly Peter is very suspicious. He thought to himself, "Did Brady do something already? He did say that he will inform him if he decided to not live a straight life." One of the policemen walked towards Peter. Peter saw this and walked out of the garage towards the policeman. He wanted to know first-hand if there was any problem.

"Hello Des, how are you?" Des, the police officer replied, "I am good Peter, how are you keeping?" Peter looked at Des in sadness but remained quiet. His grief was perceptible in his silence.

Des continued. 'I came to tell you that the man who was responsible for Joe's death has surrendered. He was drunk that day. He will stand trial. No one can bring Joe back, but he is very apologetic about his carelessness. Peter is sad. "What is the point in him being apologetic? Joe is dead," he replied.

Des explained to him, "I know Peter that you feel that way now. But for the impact of the collision; if Joe had survived, he would have had lots of problems to deal with physically and psychologically." Peter thought for some time. He thanked Des for saying that. "I was angry and thinking about my loss alone. I did not think of what Joe would have gone through. Guess, I was being selfish! Joe will never have wanted that" he said.

Des consoled him. "Sometimes we cannot see beyond our own grief. It is only human". Peter agreed, "Yes I see that now". Des enquired about the other man who was working in the garage. Peter smiled and looked back at Brady, "No he is new here. His name is Brady". Peter signalled to Brady to come close. Brady walked over to them. Peter introduced the two of them, "Brady, this is police officer Desmond. He is my school mate." Brady extended his hand. "Hello, I am Brady". Des shook Brady's hand and asked him how he was?

Brady replied that he was fine. He was just released from prison and that he was enjoying his time working for Peter. Desmond was curious, "Have you gone around town? Have you seen the sights? There is a beautiful waterfall in the hills". Peter began to laugh. "Des, I admire and share your passion for our village; but you have to remember that he works for me. Do you think he has time to go anywhere?" Des replied sheepishly "No guess not".

Brady smiled. "Peter is a hard task master but a very fair man. He did bring me out to see the waterfall and we had a picnic there. But we are content to stay at home during the weekends." Des shook his hands with both of them. "Okay, Brady. Hope Peter gives you enough time to enjoy your stay in our small town. See you around." He turned towards Peter, "Peter, I will see you soon."

Both Peter and Brady went back to the garage. Des walked back to the patrol car. The other policeman kept watching the pair of them going back to the shed. The policeman Des, who was speaking to Peter and Brady, said to his colleague. "Nothing unusual has happened here. He has not been out of town and no one has visited him." The other policeman cried out in frustration. "Where is he hiding?"

Jason is sitting on a chair in his room. He is gazing out of the window. This is one of his ways of passing the time. His attention is drawn to a man who is walking his dog. He was a thin man and was struggling to control the dog to keep him on the footpath. The stupid dog just kept walking everywhere else except for the footpath! Jason roared his head off in laughter. The road was empty now. He picked up his cold drink and took a sip. Another man came walking by. He was using crutches. "He may have been involved in a motor accident" he thought to himself. He next saw a lady who was pushing a baby in the pram. There was a young girl walking with her. She was holding on to the pram and skipping along the path chatting animatedly to her mother. Her braided hair was flying around in response to the shaking of her head. The trio stopped at the ice-cream van. The girl bought a cone ice-cream. The baby held his hand out to the van with a smile. He was jumping up and down in his buggy with excitement. The lady bought a small lolly for the baby boy. She paid for the purchases and then they walked ahead. The girl began to skip again and tried to lick the ice cream at the same time. Her mother tried to slow her down. She took a bite and began to skip again. Jason thought out aloud. "Oh, Oh! this is not going to end well." The girl took a big step and the dollop of ice cream fell to the ground. The cone was still in her hand. The girl's mouth was wide open like an 'O'.

Her brother also looked down at the ice-cream in surprise. He could not comprehend how the cone was still in his sister's hand and yet the ice-cream was on the floor. Jason chuckled in delight. He felt sorry for the girl, but the scene was so comical! He followed their progress and they reached the car park. The girl was terribly upset. The mother kneeled down beside her and consoled her. Her big blue eyes were wet, but she was a brave lass. She was not crying but, her mother knew that she was upset. She encouraged her daughter to get in the car. Then she settled the baby in the car seat. The lady got into the driver's seat and drove away. A car pulled up to the same spot and the person from the passenger seat got out and opened the rear passenger door. A man got out with a briefcase in his hand. Jason was amused. "Getting chauffeured is one thing but bringing an assistant around to wait upon! Who does that in this day and age?" Jason had to shield his eyes suddenly. He tried to see what was the cause? Something was reflecting off that briefcase. He looked at the reflection carefully. The briefcase looked very familiar. He squinted his eyes and looked again. The sticker with the symbol of the 'Green eyed monster' was staring at him. "That is too much of a coincidence" he said to himself. He looked up at the man holding the briefcase. Suddenly Jason's happy mood evaporated. He began to get palpitations. He got up from his chair and leaned on the sill to take a closer look. He looked at the man's face again. He was seeing someone that he had seen in another situation.

Bob was the person who was chauffeured and was now standing on the kerb. Suddenly Jason was very angry. He despised the fact that this man made him feel vulnerable. He had heard his whole exchange with the men in the boat. "There is honor even among thieves. But this man was beyond that. In that exchange he had shown his true colors" Jason said to himself. "This man has to pay for what he had done to him and the two men in the boat. "Oh, will it be a sweet revenge on his part?" But the man will get a shock which he will never be able to forget in his life. He will see the real Jason.

Bob and his associate walked to the bank. Jason waited for some time. After what felt like a long interval to him, Bob and Monty walked out of the door of the bank. The briefcase was not in his hand anymore. Where did he keep it? Bob surveyed the car park and the surrounding area and also up at the hotel. Jason quickly pulled himself away. He knew for sure that he was not seen when he was on the 'Marissa' but a life time of dodging the police had instilled this instinct in him. Bob got into the car when the assistant opened the car door for him. Jason looked out of the window again. The car was now driving away on the coastal road. Jason came to a decision. Until now; escaping the clutches of the police was his only target. Now he had another agenda!

Jason got on the bus next day and took a window seat. He wanted to enjoy the scenery. He sat and observed the passengers who were getting in. He had begun to recognise a few faces but he kept to himself. He did not know their names. Neither did he want to know. He was whiling away his time till the police got a bigger fish to fry. The bus sped off and Jason settled in his seat properly and looked outside. Houses and fields passed by occasionally. It took two hours for the bus to reach its intended destination which was a town named *Gotrana*.

He got out after all the other passengers had alighted. He was sporting his artificial beard. He had curled his hair as much as he could. He had also donned his sunglasses and a hat. He walked slowly around the city. He had checked his appearance in the mirror before commencing his journey and had known that no one will recognise him. He took the street that he knew will lead him to the Playmate

Pub. Suddenly he heard the wail of the police siren coming from behind him. He became very alert; but, continued to walk casually. He walked into the pub and addressed the bar tender. He stood at an angle to the door. His peripheral vision was focussed on the road. The police car pulled slightly towards the side of the pub, made a U-turn and pulled over at the kerb on the other side of the road. Both the policemen, who were in the car exited and walked into the building across from the pub.

Inside the bar, Jason ordered a beer and asked the bartender to send it to the table. He paid for his drink and a descent tip. He went down to the bottom half of the pub and carefully chose a window seat. The pub's back wall was to his back. The window was on his right side and the bartender's counter was ahead of him in the distance.

Another man walked in and sat down two tables ahead of him. He asked the bartender if he knew what was going on? The bartender told him that he had no idea but could be a possible robbery. A second man who walked in, joined in on the conversation. He had heard the tail end of the bartender's sentence and generously provided back up information. He was delighted that he was the contributor of a juicy tale. "Oh, I have just arrived from there. Two men were engaged in a fight resulting in a serious injury to one. He is critically ill. The other man has disappeared. The police were looking for people who had witnessed the incidence and were trying to question as many people as possible."


Jason had his full attention on the group. He suddenly heard a noise He looked back to see that the waitress had kept the beer glass on the table. Jason smiled up at her. "Thank you". The waitress smiled impersonally at Jason and acknowledged his thanks. Jason looked at her and said with a broad smile, "Maryland fair is very exciting". The waitress looked up at Jason's face. Her eyes grew wide in recognition and she smiled in pure pleasure. "Maryland fair is very exciting". Suddenly, Jason became very stiff. The waitress looked to the front of the house to check what had caused his smile to disappear. There were two policemen at the top, speaking to the bartender. One of the policemen was asking the bartender, "What time did you arrive to the pub today?" The bartender replied that he had arrived at ten in the morning as always; but he was at the back of the building. "I prepare the food in the kitchen at the back". Jason had become tensed because he had seen the second policeman walk down the aisle looking carefully at the individual faces. He got up from his table and pulled the waitress towards him in a bear hug. At the same time, he kept an eye on the police officer.

He hugged the waitress for a long time. One other couple were kissing each other at the back of the pub. The policeman saw this from the top and smiled. He turned back after listening to the bartender's response and saw that both Jason and the waitress were not there anymore! He returned his attention to the bartender. The waitress went into the utility area and piled up the dishes to be washed by another girl. "Anna, I am going on my break. Do you want me to help you before I leave?" she asked. She liked this young girl. She was new to the job and was a bit slow. But she made up for it by her sense of humour.

The young girl looked up at her and smiled "No I will be fine Veronica, thanks. Go and enjoy your break. You are always helping everyone else out. You deserve your time off as well." Veronica smiled and went out to the smoking shed. She sat down for a few minutes and hugged herself. It had been a while since she had seen or touched Jason. He was in disguise, that is why she couldn't recognise him. He looked so handsome despite his beard. 'Maryland' was their usual password whenever Jason was in trouble.

She slipped her hand into the pocket of her skirt and brought her cigarette case out. Another piece of neatly folded paper slipped out of her pocket and fell to the floor. She looked at it curiously. She bent down to pick it up. She unfolded the paper and looked at it. She did not have it prior to Jason visiting her. She was absolutely certain. There was a poem written on the paper along with an address.

'The big daddy bobs his head,

Always likes to be admired.

bow to him and,

you will feel blessed'


She lit up her cigarette and smoked. Who was big daddy? Where can she find him? She looked at the address. She will begin the searching at the stated address, but she can't approach the house directly. She continues to contemplate. What is the reward? She has no clue, but she will do what Jason has asked her to do. She began to plan her strategy.

## CHAPTER 6: NOVEMBER 10th 08:00

A knock could be heard at the door. Jimmy looked up at the wall clock from his arm chair. Eight at night! Who might it be? He was not expecting anyone. Whoever it is, will go away if he did not respond, he thought to himself. He settled back in his chair to read the book he was engrossed in. The knocking was now an octave higher. Frustrated, Jimmy puts his book down on the table. He might as well answer it; or there will be no peace. Looks like the person was stubborn! Now there was a heavy pounding on the door. But Jimmy was also a stubborn man. He took his time to open the door. He stepped out on to the vestibule and opened the outside door. He saw two police men standing outside. Jimmy frowned. What happened now? "Hello officers, what can I do for you?" he enquired politely. The policeman asked him if he could enter. Jimmy was not very pleased to see them, but he had no choice. "Of course! I will get some tea for you?" He said with a sweet saccharin smile. One of the policemen answered him very rudely. "You don't have to be sarcastic Jimmy. We just want to check the house". Jimmy moved aside slightly. The officer passed him by and went in to the house. The policeman who stood at the door step, engaged Jimmy in a conversation. "What are you doing for a living these days?" Jimmy looked at him as if he was a headless no a brainless in this case, monster. "Oh nothing, I am just doing odd jobs." The policeman asked him if he had met some of his other prison inmates. Jimmy replied in the negative. Jimmy is annoyed. He frowned. "Sure, they did not come for a casual visit in the middle of the night". He was definite that someone was up to something and that is why he was getting a visit. There was more to this visit than what was being demonstrated. The other policeman came back after searching the house. He shrugged his shoulders to the policeman who was waiting with Jimmy and indicated that all was clear.

The policeman at the door said goodbye to Jimmy while the other one waited a few meters away near the car. "Take care Jimmy. Don't get into any trouble". Jimmy's saccharin coated smile was firmly back in place. "Sure, whatever you say officer, goodnight" The two policemen got into the car and drove away. Jimmy stood at the threshold for a little while. Did someone get into any trouble? Did Jason escape as he had promised the night before they parted? He would have heard from Jason if he had been granted parole. Jimmy sighed, "I will know soon enough". Jimmy went in and closed the door after him. He left the room window open and left the large light switched on purposefully. He knew that they will come back to check again when he was unaware. Let them look all they want! "If Jason did escape; he will not go anywhere near his friends' houses" he concluded. His mood for reading had evaporated. He might as well go to sleep.


The main street of *Clapa Gopolini* was alive with people. It was the feast day of their patron saint. There will be a procession from the church in the evening. The shops held discounted sales on the day; in reverence for their patron saint. The streets were very busy and crowded again today. Bob's car had just extricated itself from the traffic and was traveling on the coastal road. There were plenty of cars traveling in that direction. The exit lanes on either side engulfed the cars as soon as it turned into the lane. Eventually the number of cars on the coastal road continued to shrivel. They kept disappearing like the sand filtering through the fingers! Bob's car and one another car were on the road now. The second car which was blue in color, overtook Bob's white car and sped away. Bob's car kept going and ultimately reached his villa. The electronic gates opened, and the car was driven in by the chauffeur.

The blue car now returned back to the neighbourhood of Bob's villa. Veronica got out. She looked around at all the villas in the vicinity. She checked the address that Jason had given to her. The next villa should be the one, she thought to herself. She walked back to her car. She picked up a few things from the car; a water bottle, a camera, a pen, a note pad and a pair of binoculars. Veronica locked the car and walked in the direction of Bob's villa. She behaved like a casual visitor. She saw a tree near Bob's front door at a far distance. She will not be seen from here. She went over to the tree and climbed up the branches. She selected a thick flat branch and settled herself comfortably. The branches were nice and broad. She kept her notepad and the camera on the nearby branch. The binocular was hanging around her neck. She looked up at the villa through her binoculars. The villa was huge and circular in design, white in color with a blue trim and had two floors. There was a balcony on the first floor. A colorful awning shielded the occupants from the rays of the sun. Bob was seated on a rattan chair. His two assistants were standing on the balcony. There was a tray with teapot and a few cups on the table. Veronica took out her camera and began to photograph the scene. A beautiful girl in a bikini came out and gave a cigar to Bob. Once he kept the cigar in his mouth, she lighted it. She then went back inside after collecting the now empty tray on her way. Monty dialled a number and spoke into the phone. "Hello," Monty said into the phone. "Big daddy wants to speak to you". He listened to the person on the other side. He gave the phone to Bob. "Hello, Bob here." Veronica began to lip read.

"Ah! So, this was Bob; the big daddy". Monty went over to the edge of the balcony and looked around. He saw a car driving up the road in the distance and looked at it. The car drew close to the villa. Monty kept looking at the car. He saw Marty at the wheels behind the windscreen. The guard looked up in inquiry. Monty indicated to the security guard to open the door. The security guard obeyed and let the car through.

Veronica kept clicking away on her camera. She could follow the pattern of the lips through the lens. Marty got out of the car and went up to the first floor of the villa. Veronica looked up to the balcony. She had taken enough photographs so, she kept the camera away and looked through the binoculars. Marty appeared on the balcony. Bob was still on the phone. Marty came close and shook Bob's hands. Bob indicated to him to sit down. Marty kept his suitcase on the floor. Bob finished his conversation and looked at Marty. Veronica continued to watch through the binoculars.

Bob nodded his head at Monty who in return, signalled to the other guard. The guard went in and after a while, came out with a tray in his hands. The tray had two glasses and a bottle of alcohol. He set the tray down on the table beside Bob. He served the alcohol in two glasses and handed one to Bob. Then he gave the other glass to Marty. Bob asked Marty "How are you?" Marty thanked him and took a sip. He looked at the bottle and praised the quality of the alcohol. "Wow, this spirit is excellent. You have great taste. I am good thank you". Bob was very pleased. The quality of the alcohol indicated the extent of his wealth. It was a very expensive brand.

Marty indicated to the suitcase. "I have the merchandise for you." Bob asked him, "What happened in Africa?" Marty explained that the Secret Service had kept the raid operation a complete secret. The staff who were employed by the SS but were in their payroll were also not aware! He said that thankfully, one of his partners took the blame and went to jail leaving his family in the care of the other partners. On the other hand, taking advantage of the raid; Tommy had stolen the diamonds they had kept hoarded for so long. That was their life savings. They were going to sell the whole lot at the next black market auction on 1st of February.

Marty sighed as he lifted up the suitcase from the floor and extended it to Bob. Monty took it from Marty's hands at a signal from his boss. Monty gave Marty an envelope in return which he looked at with suspicion. However, he took it in his hand and opened it. The envelope contained a few photographs. Marty looked at it and his eyes became wide like saucers. Suspicion gave way to disbelief and pain. "Oh my God, what happened? How did the police get wind of this?"


Bob apologised to Marty and explained that the police got there before them. Tommy and his associate were killed in the crossfire. Marty kept looking at the photos again and again in disbelief. Veronica could also see the photos through the binoculars. It showed Tommy and Augustine lying dead on the floor. A few policemen in uniforms were seen in the photograph 'working on the scene'. A 'do not cross' tape was tied around the trawler, on the deck. There was a newspaper cutting in the envelope which reported about the siege of the diamonds and the death of Tommy and his bodyguard, Augustine.

It also reported that the police had found a clue in the trawler which will lead to Tommy's partners. Marty is beside himself with grief. "Everything is destroyed. Our life savings are all gone; and the European police are after us now! What will we do? I don't even have money to restart my life over once again. I am doomed".

Bob consoled Marty and apologised again for being late. He also added that they could have saved Tommy and the diamonds only if they were there an hour earlier. Marty exploded, "Who cares about Tommy? He showed us his true colors! Why will I even care for him? I am more worried about the diamonds leaving our hands. That was our life savings".

Bob leaned over and patted Marty's shoulders. Monty handed over the suitcase that the young woman brought from one of the rooms. "The fees for the counterfeit notes is in this briefcase here. I have added some more extra bundles to it". Marty looked at the suitcase and thanked Bob with all his heart, "Thanks Bob. You are a true friend. What would I have done if you had not been so kind?" Bob humbly waved Marty's gratitude aside. "Don't worry, you look after yourself and start your life over". Marty picked up the suitcase and headed out the door. He went down to his car. His shoulders were stooped over. He suddenly looked ten years older than what he had looked half an hour ago. He got into his car and without even a backward glance drove out through the gates.

Monty followed Marty's car with his eyes for a long distance. He then looked back at Bob and smiled. "Problem solved. He swallowed it whole". Bob just smiled. "No big deal, I am just three hundred million richer" he thought to himself.

Veronica was flabbergasted at this exchange. Jason had told her that Bob and his men had killed Tommy and his associate. How did Bob produce the photographs of the police being involved in this? "Wait till Jason hears this! I wonder what is going to be his reaction?" Veronica thought to herself. She knew that there was no need to know anything further. So, she got down from the tree and drove home.

A police car drove around the bend in the road and approached the police station. It drove into the gates and halted at the front door. A few officers got out of the car and walked in to the building. They entered the conference room which was nearly full. They walked up to the top of the room and sat down at the chairs that were vacant. The Chief of Police walked in. Everyone had their attention on the chief now. Chief Parker began, "Good morning. What is the agenda for today?" The Police constable mentioned the robbery in a trader's apartment at the North side of the district. They discussed this for a while. Next, he reported that there was a repeat APB on Jason Jazz. The chief asked the men and women to keep looking. "Check out anyone related to him, especially his ex-prison mates" he thundered.


Jason's ex-prison mates were all holed up in a pub at the far end of the city. Jimmy, Brady, David and Lucas were sitting around a table. There was a picture of the pub from the olden days painted on its modern wall. The fire was roaring in the fire place. A waitress walked in with four pints of beer in her hand. She kept them down on the table and looked up at the men with a smile. "Lads, can I get you anything else?" Jimmy looked around to check if anyone wanted anything and answered for all of them, "That's it for the moment sweetie. We will let you know".  The waitress swanned away from the table. The men picked up the glasses and raised in salute. "Here's to our life of freedom and peace"

Everyone drank thirstily. Then they kept their pint glasses down. Jimmy looked at all of them one by one. He saw tiredness in all their faces. He wondered what the problem was? David was the first one to blurt out at the slightest provocation. He was unhappy living with his parents. They were very reproachful about their boys visit to the prison. They were the subject of ridicule amongst the extended family and friends. Lucas gave out that the problems actually doubled; when the police presented themselves to their house.

Jimmy asked, "I wonder if you know that two of them are outside the pub even now?" He continued, "They are ready to spring into immediate action if necessary." Lucas looked at him in surprise. "Jimmy! Are you sure about that?" Jimmy answered in the affirmative, "Yes I have been watching them since I arrived. They all looked at each other. Brady who was in a sombre mood dragged them back to the conversation. He was happy living with Peter temporarily but, "I am actually getting bored now". Jimmy was unhappy because he was not finding much work. Had he not owned the house; it would have been difficult for him to survive! All of them wanted to behave until the police were watching them and then be free to live as they pleased. Their conversation ultimately turned towards Jason and whether he had escaped. The policemen turning up at their doors conveyed that he may have escaped but he himself had not contacted them. That would be Jason's very nature as observed by Jimmy in the prison. He was the closest to Jason and yet Jason never imposed on him for anything. They continued to sit there and talk until closing time and then walked out of the pub. It was the first time for them; the dinner bell had not rung to end their conversation. Jimmy was now worried about where Jason was, if he was safe and what was he doing?

## CHAPTER 7: NOVEMBER 12th  23:00

This street was enveloped in darkness. The houses that were lined on either side of the street were unlit as well; with the one exception. The light was shining through the window of this bungalow which was sitting beside the canal. The light was casting a large shadow. The kitchen window was open, and noises of dishes being kept away could be heard. The person doing the chores was humming to herself. She finished tidying up the kitchen. She then went to the living room and tidied up the seats. She looked at the items on the mantlepiece and dusted them one by one. There were no family photos. The house when unoccupied would have provided no clue about the inhabitants of this house.  She had arranged the objects in their proper positions, placed the fire door back on the fireplace. The wood had finished burning and the house which was well insulated was warm and cosy. The heat will last until eight or nine in the morning. She checked to ensure that the doors and windows were locked and turned out the lights as she went from room to room. She eventually reached the bedroom.

Jason was sitting at the table. The passport that was nearly finished was resting on the top of the table. The page with his photograph was open and a paper weight was weighing it down on to the passport. The name on the passport was 'Shears'. He was now preparing an address proof with the help of the computer. She went near him and kept her hands on his shoulder.

Jason smiled. Veronica bent down and kissed Jason on the top of his head. He leaned back into her and closed his eyes. "You smell very nice." Veronica laughed but continued to massage his shoulders, "Is that true? I was becoming a little bit jealous of the hotel you were staying in?" Jason looked at her. His eyes were dancing. "I could show you in various ways; that you have no reason to be jealous of the hotel or anyone else". She bent down further and kissed him on the lips. Jason laughed, "You are the most precious thing in the world to me. I will go to the ends of the world; just to keep you safe". She exerted some more pressure on his shoulders and urged him to get up. He got up from the table after switching off the computer and the table lamp. He reminded her that he will need to stay in the hotel for some more time. Veronica forbade him to speak about it any further. She did not want to know. She wanted to just live one day at a time. They both went and lay down on the bed facing each other. Jason gathered Veronica very close to him and kissed her deeply on the lips. Veronica sighed with longing. She was happy that he had come back to her even if it was temporary. He lifted up the spread from the bed, turned off the light and pulled the bedspread over the two of them. The room and the house were now enveloped in darkness just like the rest of the houses on the street. Only the dogs barking in the distance and the occasional screeching of a cat could be heard.

Jason was showered and ready in the morning. He looked very handsome with his blonde beard in a dark blue suit. He sat sipping his coffee. Veronica sat beside him and was having her breakfast. She was ready to go out as well. She had dressed in clothes and shoes suitable for walking. She asked him about his plans. Jason replied that he had to do some paper work. Veronica informed him that she will be in her office. Jason finished his coffee and got up from the chair. He picked up his briefcase, kissed Veronica goodbye and left the house. He had borrowed her car for the day. He drove to the town of *Clapa Gopolini*. He parked the car in the parking lot and sat down for a few minutes. He looked at the entrance to the bank. For a bank catering to the needs of a small town; it was a very busy one. Not surprisingly though! This was the poshest town in western Europe where rich people had their second homes or came to spend their holidays during the summer.

Posh people always went to the bank instead of conducting their business online. They had more opportunity to show off their wealth. The time for Jason's appointment was fast approaching. He got out of the car, locked it and walked into the bank with his briefcase. He walked up to the reception where the bank's customer service staff was waiting for him. "Mr. Shears?" she enquired in confirmation. Jason answered in the affirmative and enquired politely if he was late. She reassured him, that it was not the case and they liked their customers to feel valued. She brought him into a room and did the paper work to open a new account. She took his credentials, checked them properly and enquired his reason for choosing this particular bank. He answered appropriately to all the questions. Once the lady was satisfied, she opened an account for him. "Mr. Shears, you had requested for a locker. I will bring you back to the waiting area. The bank's assistant manager, Denise will come and escort you to the vault" she concluded.

Jason thanked her charmingly and went to the general area to wait. A few minutes later Denise, the bank's assistant manager came up to Jason and escorted him to the interior of the bank. He was assisted to open the locker.

After some time, Jason came out of the bank and went and sat in his car. He drove away and then returned to the same spot after a while. He parked his car and continued to sit there. He took out the camera and photographed the people coming in and out of the bank. At lunch time, he locked the car, went into the cafe and bought some sandwiches, a cold drink and a cup of coffee. He went back to his car and sat there munching his sandwich. The bank was closed at the moment for lunch. He had one hour to spare. He was contemplating his next move. He had to make a good plan and execute it to perfection.

Suddenly there was a loud knock on the windscreen. Jason was in shock. He slowly turned around to see a homeless person knocking on the side window. Jason rolled the glass down with irritation but, he carefully schooled his face. The homeless guy said that he was hungry.

Jason picked up the second set of sandwich and the drink and gave it to his fellow human being. The man thanked him and left. Jason nearly puked with relief. He rolled up the glass on the window back again. The camera was kept on the car seat. Thank God, it was lunchtime and he was not taking photos! He would have raised suspicion. Jason continued to wait and watch the bank until it closed down for business in the evening. He took photographs as he deemed necessary for the job. He vacated the parking lot in the evening and drove away. He began to think about Veronica as he was driving and wondered if she had made any progress.

Veronica in the meantime, had been following Bob around for part of the day. She took a taxi to the specialty coffee shop where Bob had his coffee every morning. His assistants ordered the coffee for him while Bob went and sat down on one of the tables and chatted up the waitresses. The security guards after ordering the coffee sat at another table behind him.

Today it was a waitress named Wendy who had served him. He always ensured that the girls he went out with were looked after very well. This continued even when the relationship was well and truly over. It was his policy to never go out with any woman more than once! He did not want his secrets to be revealed. Wendy was one of them. He had gone out with her in the past. She was thanking him for the holiday package to the Himalayas; when the men were ordering the coffee. Bob had paid for the vacation. He expressed general interest in the conversation. Bob enquired to Wendy about the other young waitress who was serving coffee on another table. She had captured his interest. Wendy was happy to supply the information. Veronica heard the entire conversation from two tables down. She got up from the table after finishing her coffee. She had learned enough from here. Bob also had finished his coffee. He then left the coffee shop. He went jogging in the green after that.

Veronica who knew his itinerary by rote, was already warming up for a jog in the park. If her presence attracted attention; she hoped that it will be only assumed as a coincidence. The place was actually busy for a week day. More and more people were becoming health conscious these days. Or they were so lonely in their own houses that they came out for a chat. Impoverished heirs and heiresses were always on the prowl for a suitable catch in this town. They lived in the hope that they will catch the eye of someone rich.

Bob was jogging with his friend Mason Steel. They were speaking to each other as they were jogging along. Bob enquired about Steel's family and his sister. Steel informed him that he was going on holiday to his sister's house. He in return enquired about Bob's plans. Bob told him of his trip to his resort in Florida for the Thanks giving day. Steel had a mischievous smile, "Are you going on your own?" Bob laughed, "Yes, this time it will be by myself. It is a strictly working holiday." Bob concluded his jogging and left the green when his assistant handed him the phone as there was a caller on the other end. Veronica was tired. She needed a drink after that exercise. That man could walk fast! She was finding it very difficult to keep up with him.

She walked up to the kiosk and purchased a bottle of water and a protein bar. She sat down on the park bench. After taking a few sips from the bottle, she sat there nibbling on the bar and thinking. She reflected on the conversation between Bob and the other man. She had some sort of idea as to what she will be required to do next. But she did not know if Jason will see it in the same manner. He always wanted to keep her safe. She thought back to her conversation with Jason the other night. He was actually surprised when he heard how Bob had cheated Marty as well. He was not expecting the piece of news that Veronica had given to him. They had compared notes. She had mentioned the photos showing police involvement in Tommy and his assistant's death.

Jason was confident that there were no police around at the time in the harbour. After their lengthy discussion long into the night, they came to the conclusion that Bob was a very unscrupulous thief who had no honor. A man who could not be trusted by anyone. A man who could go to any extent to satisfy his own needs and get what he wanted for himself. Once this conversation was over, Jason's resolve to punish Bob had strengthened further.

# CHAPTER 8: NOVEMBER 15th 20:00

The Ginger Ale pub was in the middle of the *Gotrana* City. Jimmy, Brady, David and Lucas were seated at a table. Today was the day for their rendezvous with Jason as decided before they had parted in the prison. They were excited and chatting animatedly. There is an aura of nervous energy around them. The pints have been ordered. Brady wanted to order five pints but Jimmy dissuaded him from doing so. Knowing Jason, he knew that probably Jason is already seated in the pub somewhere; he will have ordered his own pint by now!

Jason who had occupied another table in a corner; very near to them smiled when he heard Jimmy's response. He had been a very good friend and he was still the same. Jimmy always quoted the proverb, 'Out of sight, out of mind' whenever Brady complained about his wife. But as far as Jimmy was concerned; Jason will always be in his mind, even if he was out of sight. Jason waited for a long time listening to them speak to each other. He then drew their attention to him.

'Hello guys', Brady turned around with a broad smile. Jason indicated to him to not speak by keeping his fingers on his lips. Brady kept his mouth clamped shut but his eyes were dancing with joy. Jimmy was grinning wide and David and Lucas smiled. Jason asked them how the newly reformed members of the society were doing? The men scooted around closer and made space for him. Jason looked out of the window. The policeman was not there anymore. He probably got fed up of waiting and watching. He then moved over to the table where the men were seated.

He could now see the window directly. Lucas could not stop staring at Jason. "Oh my God, you really escaped" he blurted. Jason laughed at Lucas' expression. They all wanted to know how he managed to escape from the prison. Jason described the adventure he had undertaken; but his expression was very sober. They all remained quiet even after he had finished speaking. They were aware of the peril, Jason had been through. And it was not over. He was still in hiding. He could not do normal things the way they were able to do in their lives.

The police were still raiding the men's houses continuously. David and Lucas had to move out from their parents' home because of that. They were living a very minimalistic life, hardly able to keep their heads above water. Jason consoled them and asked them to bear with him for a month. Jimmy admired Jason's beard. "I love your beard man! It makes you look very suave. How come you did not keep a beard in prison?" Jason laughed and answered, "Isn't it good that I had not sported a beard in prison!"

Brady wanted to know what Jason had up his sleeve? Jason answered that if they were happy to be satisfied with the bare minimum details; then, he will explain what he had in his mind. The men all nodded in agreement to his condition. Jason informed them, "With your help, I am going to rob a bank!" They all looked at him as if he had suddenly grown horns. Other than Jason's skills in armoured van robbery, the expertise in robbing banks was zero on the ground. Jimmy and David were the white-collar criminals. They did not even touch money with their bare hands! The computer did the job for them. Although for fun; they prided in calling themselves the gentlemen robbers! Brady asked, "Jason, do you really mean it? You are not even out of the woods yet; and you want to do a bank job now?"

Jimmy cautiously asked Jason's plan and what was the reward at the end? Jason told them that whatever will be obtained will be split into equal shares among all the partners. David had reservations as he began to guess that Jason had no clue to the amount that they were going to rob. He did not want to risk his and his brother's neck for a pittance. Even if by a minute, he was the older of the two. Lucas' wellbeing was his responsibility.

Lucas also obeyed his brother with his eyes closed. He may slag the rest of them but never questioned David's decisions. Jason asked them all to keep their reservations on hold. He told them that while he was trying to escape, he got involved in an incident in which a large sum of money was involved. He had already formulated a rough plan as to how to rob the bank. With the help of his friends, he could really make it work!

The men stared at him. It was beyond their comprehension that Jason will come up with such a lackadaisical plan! After a while, David opted-in. Lucas looked at him as if he was really seeing his brother for the first time; his loyalty to his brother was stronger than his own reservations and so he kept quiet. Jimmy and Brady would have joined in nevertheless. Once satisfied with their level of commitment; Jason brought out an envelope from his coat pocket. He again reminded them that they have to follow his instructions to the letter. He warned them of the consequence of not being careful. The men shivered at the thought of another stint in prison and they all promise to be careful.

They are all  serious now and concentrating on his words. They are back in the business. All the back slapping and flippant conversation is now over. Jason turned to Lucas and asked him if he can make a hand gun with a silencer. "You have to personally make it and not purchase it." Lucas agreed. Everyone looked at Jason with suspicion. He reassured them that it is for his own safety and not for the job. The men relaxed only slightly; but kept quiet. They could not bear to see Jason going back to prison or getting killed. The level of the threat and seriousness had suddenly increased with the inclusion of the gun in the plot They knew that Jason will kill himself first; and not rat on his friends. This was the purpose of the gun. If the situation seemed hopeless; he will kill himself. Jason looked at David and handed over six photographs to him. "These are the photographs of the security guards working in the bank. I need you to find out their activities". David consented to do the job.

He then turned to Jimmy. He gave him a photo and waited for his expression. Jimmy chuckled. Brady remarked "Jimmy, looks like you are going to really enjoy the job you have been assigned". Jimmy answered, "Oh yes!" He was handed over assistant manager Denise' photo. She was a charming woman and the reason for Jimmy's delight. He smiled, he knows what Jason wanted him to do.

Brady is waiting eagerly for his chore. He gets the photograph of Theodore Williams, the bank manager. He frowned at the photo and then moaned. "Jason you don't love me as much as you love Jimmy. That is why you gave me this bearded fellow". But he knew that Jason has a purpose in allocating him this job. Jason also understood that Brady does not really mean anything with the moaning. He asked Brady if he can raise some money for the venture. Brady declined because he didn't want to steal cars and be caught. Also, he did not want to break Peter's trust while he was living under his roof.

He will be happy to live on whatever he gets from what Jason repeatedly refers to as 'the accidental heist'. It didn't matter even if it was prison life that he got at the end of it. Jason complied but asked the entire group to come up with options to raise money. Jason also asked them to meet him back in twenty days. They had to meet David individually by day fifteen. He again reminded them, the importance of being careful and vigilant.

All of them with the exception of Jimmy left the party in one's and two's. Jimmy and Jason sat across from each other. Jimmy looked at Jason in the eye and asked him what his plan was? Jason explained that he wanted to rob the vault of this bank. He believed that there are a few hundred million inside those lockers. Jimmy is astounded that he had involved all of them on a wild goose chase. "Jason! Are you mad? What are you trying to prove?"

Jason reassured him that he was not trying to prove anything. He had laid a plan where, if anyone got caught; it would be only him. The rest will be free to live their life as before. Jason also gave him an option "You are free to walk away even now if you want; and so are the others". But Jimmy refused to walk away. "I have full trust in you Jason. I just worry about the lads". Jason told him to calm down and let the lads decide for themselves.

They decide to go to the casino to play a few games. Jason always had a lucky hand and he was well disguised. If they were not able to recognise him; the police will definitely find it difficult. The casino he was bringing Jason to; had the reputation of being happy to host 'respectable gentlemen' like them. They walked out of the pub in a happy and contended frame of mind. They had ironed out their differences of opinion. They can and will now, face the world together.

Brady got up in the morning in the hotel room. He lay in bed reflecting on yesterday evening and the past few weeks. He had asked Peter for a few days off. Peter had seen Brady's boredom increasing so he was not surprised at the request when it came. He now understood Brady's problem. All the time he had worked in the garage, he never looked at any of the cars with greed or longing. But he always checked out the security system in the car. It was the highly prohibitionary nature symbolised by the hi-tech system that drove him to try and jeopardise it. He had this urge to prove to the world that he could breach any security system in the world. It could be boiled down to attention seeking; an act of childishness. Brady had laughed disbelievingly when Peter had said this to him. But when he processed the information, he knew that what Peter had said was true. May have been because he was an orphan. He grew up in an institution where he was one among the many! This analysis helped him boost his self-confidence. Living with Peter had provided him with a sense of stability. He had been a distraction for Peter while he worked out his grief. They had helped each other out in their mutual need. It was time to move on. They both knew that they had different principles and outlook of life. May have been a result of upbringing. Peter was born and lived in a stable family environment whereas; Brady was brought up in the turbulence of the orphanage.

He sat up from the bed and got ready. The bank opened at half eight. He groaned. Who made the rule that this bank should open so early when everywhere else in Europe, banks opened at ten in the morning? "Anyway, laziness will not get me anywhere" he thought to himself. He ate his breakfast in the hotel. He had hired a car yesterday in *Gotrana*. He drove out to the city of *Clapa Gopolini* and to the address given by Jason. He parked in the car park. There was another ten minutes for the bank to open. He sat in the car exactly where Jason had parked a few days ago. It was entirely coincidental. It worked as a good spot for prolonged surveillance.

The bank was directly in front of him. The main gate and the side gate, both were visible. He also had a good view of the surrounding area which may help in the long run. He was not going to get out of the car today. He will observe all he can first. At twenty past eight a man walked to the side door of the bank. He opened it and went inside. He could now see that the lights were turned on inside the building. Another car now drove in through the side gate. "There is probably a car park at the back" he surmised to himself. The third car went inside. More and more cars kept driving in. He could not see the occupants of the car. He will bring a binocular tomorrow; he promised himself.

David, who had worked with his eyes over the lens of a microscope all his life; had a binocular with him. He had zeroed in on the person opening the side gate, the same time as Brady had. He had spotted his quarry; well at least one of them! He had six to follow. In fairness, Jason had done half of the work for him. A good mark of a great leader! Send your soldier armed with at least some information. He can find out the rest.

David and Brady stayed in their original posts until the evening. David left for *Gotrana* but Brady followed the bank manager Theodore Williams to his home. He drove further and parked a good distance away. He then walked back to the area where the bank manager's house was. He saw a woman leave the house as soon as the bank manager arrived. Mr. Williams was sitting at the porch and a small girl was waving at the woman who was leaving. The house was just one hour away from the bank. He will have to come back tomorrow to observe further. He went back to *Gotrana.*

Lucas had booked a dormitory for them. They were going to pose as tourists. *Gotrana* was famous for its white sandy beaches and was a popular destination for the wealthy from the cooler climes in the northern hemisphere. This meant that crime rate was also high. They will be able to hide in plain sight. They had now decided to stay together to minimise costs. Escaping the watchful eyes of the police and traveling within Europe was not difficult. When they don't turn up to sign for parole, they will be missed but now they are in a different country altogether. They asked Lucas about his day.

While the others were on surveillance, Lucas was out and about looking for hardware shops of a particular kind. It was a new city to him, but he liked the sense of adventure. The thrill of sussing out shops that engaged in shady deals was well within his comfort zone. He went from shop to shop and procured inexpensive but good quality raw materials needed for the manufacture of a gun. Finding them was difficult; however, it added to his sense of bravado.

Jimmy was in his own home. He had decided to begin his work slowly. He had only one person to follow. The four of them disappearing together will be a cause for concern. David and Lucas were twins so it was understood that they will go everywhere together. Brady had no fixed abode; he was technically free to live anywhere he liked. He himself can leave in a couple of days. At least if the police came looking, one of them will be above suspicion. That will take the attention away from Jason and his other friends.

Brady woke up the next morning at around five. He got ready and went straight to the estate of the bank manager's residence. He went around the house and looked closely. It was dark. It was a two storey house with porticoes all around. The post supporting the slate roof was covered with 'Devil's eye' on one side. The vine was very strong. The room on the top floor was brightly lit. The manager was probably getting ready. He needed to be out of the house for half seven to reach the bank by half eight. Brady went back to his car and waited. He could see the house from where he was parked. The estate was coming alive. People were leaving their houses for work. The voices of the older children could be heard now. The house keeper arrived at the house. She opened the door with her own keys. Brady kept waiting.

The manager came out of the house, got into his car and drove away. He followed the bank manager to the bank.  He waited till the manager came out in the evening. He then followed him back to his house. After seeing the bank manager safely in and waiting until dark, Brady drove back to *Gotrana*. He reported his achievements to the lads. It was a little bit boring and he needed some more action. Here he felt that he was not in control at all.

David had gone back to the bank in the morning. He noted that the same pattern from yesterday was repeated but it was a different security guard that was on duty today. He now knew that there are two security guards on duty at every shift. There was only one shift. It began at eight in the morning and finished at six in the evening. He had found four of his quarries by now. He needed to see two more and then decide on a course of action.

Lucas was still working away on his gun. Jimmy had joined them this evening. He had a more productive day. He had followed the Assistant Bank manager cum vault in charge to the coffee shop at around ten thirty-five. She went into the coffee shop and purchased two artisan coffees, a dough nut and a croissant wrapped in individual bags. She went to the milk counter, mixed one coffee with sweetener and the other one with two sachets of sugar. She then kept the coffee cups on a tray and turned around to take some paper towels. She then left with her purchases and went into the bank through the side door. He was going to follow her again the next day. "She is very pleasing to the eyes" he remarked to the boys. They looked at each other and then jumped on Jimmy who was stretched on the bed. They tousled around for a good while.

Brady went to the bank manager's house in the morning. He waited for him to come out of the house. After a while, he saw a school bus pull up at the kerb. The young girl came out of the house with the house keeper and got into the school bus. The manager waved good bye to his daughter from the top floor of the house. The bank manager then got ready and went to the bank. Brady again followed the manager to work.

The bank manager came out of the bank in his car in the evening. "It looks like Denise is with him. Wonder where they are off to?" Brady thought to himself. He followed them. Mr. Williams had offered a lift to Denise. She lived near his daughter's school. He was going to pick her up this evening. Denise had thanked him. It was ideal. Mr. Williams asked her "Which restaurant are you going to go to this evening Denise?" "Clive's food galore," she replied. He nodded his head in approval. She had good taste. "It is an expensive place, but has class," She agreed. She was going out with her friends. "It is my best friend's hen night," she revealed to him. "Aah, that is why you are taking a day off tomorrow" he teased her. They had reached the school by now. Denise thanked him and got out. Brady who was still following them slowed down his car at the side of the road. Denise walked to the estate in which she owned a house. The bank manager drove into the school.

Brady followed him inside at a distance. He saw the bank manager parking the car. Mr. Williams got out, locked the car and entered the building. Brady parked at one of the slots near Mr. Williams' car. He waited there for a while. Then he got out of his car and looked around carefully. He approached Mr. Williams' car and opened it effortlessly. He checked the car thoroughly. He found Mr. Williams' phone in the dashboard. He hacked the phone and kept it back in the same place. He went back to his car and waited; then when they both came out, he followed Mr. Williams back home with his daughter. He stayed the night in the car near Mr. Williams' house. It was not at all comfortable.

Once the bank manager was up in the morning, he went back to the dormitory and slept for a couple of hours. By ten thirty, he was back outside the bank. He knew that David and Jimmy were somewhere nearby. He dared not look for them. Jason had issued strict orders.

David walked to the coffee shop. He had seen the security guard come out of the bank. He had met with a woman on his way. From their level of intimacy, it looked like they were husband and wife. They walked into the coffee shop together. When David arrived, they were already seated at a table. David chose a seat from where he could hear both of them. He went to the counter and ordered breakfast. He then went back to his chair and began to read the newspaper. "I had gone to look for some Christmas presents Tony" she said to him. "Cool babe" he replied. "Did you get something nice?" He asked her. She said that she got a few bits and pieces for stocking fillers. "You do know what Clara wants for Christmas?" she asked, looking at him seriously. "I know babe, that is what I am worried about" he said. They both sipped their coffee for a little while. Then Tony looked up with a cheerful smile, "Don't worry Babe, God will provide". The lady smiled and rubbed his cheek tenderly. "Thank you, Tony. It is your sunny disposition that keeps me going. Don't ever give that up". Tony laughed, "All right Babe, I won't. It is better to smile than to be upset. Sweetheart" he said, "You could cry all of your life and yet get nowhere". They walked out of the coffee shop together. David continued to sit there and thought for some time.

Brady followed the manager to his house and parked behind the building. He made himself comfortable for the night. Sometime later, the transmitter kept on the passenger seat began to blink. He sat up and kept the ear piece in his ears.

"Hello optician's office, Francesca speaking, answered a voice from the other end. Mr. Williams replied, "hello this is Theodore Williams from 20, Myracrise Drive". The optician recognised his name and answered with enthusiasm, "hello Mr. Williams, how are you? What can I do for you today?" He answered, "I am good Francesca. Iw Ould like to make an appointment for my annual eye check up". She paused as if checking the appointment log and then answered, "the earliest available appointment is on Thursday and there are four slots available from quarter past four to five pm; which one would you like to take?" He thought for a few seconds and then said, "okay quarter to five suits me best". She confirmed the date and the time and then disconnected the phone after wishing him a good evening.

Brady kept the ear piece down. It is time for him to act now. The waiting has paid off. He looked at the caller id. He rang the optician's office and made an appointment for himself.

Jimmy was enjoying his job thoroughly. Never in life had he so closely observed a woman. Until now, he was busy observing the rise and fall in the corporate finance world. This was a new assignment and he liked its nature. It was the same as his job in the corporate world. Wait and watch and then pounce at the right moment. He had observed her for a full week now. There was nothing much to report. She went to work in the morning. She came out to buy the coffee at the break. She stayed in the bank until closing time. She then took the public transport home. She stayed in the house the whole night. Once a week, on the Saturday; she went to the gymnasium and the supermarket. A boring life by the looks of it! It was not a very exciting life.

It is ten thirty now. He went into the coffee shop, ahead of Denise. He got into the queue and ordered two coffees. He went to the counter and added sugar and sweetener to the respective cups. Today, Denise was standing near him at the counter and was preparing her coffee. Her perfume was very exotic and erotic! Denise turned to get the hand towels, Jimmy used this opportunity and switched the cups. He walked away with the coffee and waited at an alleyway. In the evening, the boys were looking at him with eyes wide in surprise. "It's all right boys, anyone can switch cups by mistake, you know!" Jimmy laughed at then luxuriating in the moment when they looked at him in disbelief.

David now knew the rotation of the security guard. They were in teams of two and they got a two day break in between. The first group he had watched was Tony and his mate, Javier. Day two was Leone and Miguel and day three was Pinto and Terry. The first set was back on day four. The bank was closed only on Sunday, so the first team began their duty on the next Monday. David looked at his notes. Tony liked coffee and a wrap, Javier preferred a tea and a roll. They bought the standard sizes with a meat and two vegetables. One of them came out for a smoke, went to the coffee shop and bought the food. He then went back inside. Fifteen minutes later, the second guy came out and smoked. He went go back inside within five minutes or sooner if he had finished smoking sooner. Then they will not be seen until lunch time. They repeated the same process at lunch but the second guy went to the coffee shop this time. "Good policy" he thought; "only one person came out at one time while the other person held the fort. The money spent was equal, so no one was paying extra. They both got smoking breaks and fresh air as well. A well paired team!" Leone and Miguel were totally opposite. They both preferred coffee and a burger. They both took their breaks one after the other. They both ate in the coffee shop. Pinto and Terry preferred tea and rolls, but they too sat in the coffee shop at different times. These four did not smoke or have any other visible habits. "Well, that is my assignment done. Hope Jason chooses an appropriate date for whatever he has planned."

It was Thursday evening. Brady walked into the optician's office. The receptionist greeted him, "Your name sir?" Brady replied, "Jack Braveheart. I have an appointment for 1630." The receptionist replied, "Mr. Braveheart, please take a seat. One of our opticians will be with you shortly." Brady sat down and looked around. There were a good number of customers in the shop. Some were on their own and some were with children. The place was decorated with advertisements of glasses and lens. The price on most of them were inflated.

He looked towards the door. It was 1625. "Where is he? He should have been here now?" He asked himself. Just then, Mr. Williams walked in hurriedly. The receptionist looked up at him. "Sir, your name please." Mr. Williams replied, "Theodore Williams, I have an appointment for 1645. Sorry, I am late." The receptionist smiled, "Mr. Williams, please take a seat. We will be with you shortly." Just then, Brady was called in to a cubicle by an Optician. She checked his eye sight, took a picture of his eyes and checked out his retina with an ophthalmoscope. She showed him how the frames would sit on his face. Brady asked if he could take his time selecting the type of frames. The optician handed over the digital display to Brady and excused herself for a few minutes. Brady looked at the screen. He saw that the picture of his eyes and the specifications for the glasses required for him were visible on the one screen. He quickly took a picture of the display on his mobile phone and forwarded it to David. He heard a ping on his phone in a few minutes. He looked at the message and smiled. David had posted a large 'Thumbs up' symbol.

Meanwhile another optician came out of the office. "Sandra, Mr. Williams is our regular customer. I will look after him first." The bank Manager looked gratefully at the optician. "Thank you." The Optician explained to the bank manager, "Sandra is our new appointee. She is not familiar with the regular clients yet. You will not have to wait the next time." She brought him to a work table. She used the cubicle beside the one, the optician dealing with Brady was using. The optician got Mr. Williams to read the illuminated eye chart projector, took the picture of his eyes and showed him the screen to demonstrate how the glasses will sit on his eyes. He will also need a new pair of lenses for his work. They were still looking at the pictures when, Brady walked in clutching at his chest, "Sorry excuse me. Can you please get me some water? I need to take my medicine." He clutched harder at his chest and began to sway. Both the optician and the bank manager were alarmed. The optician got up quickly, "Oh please, take this seat. I will call the ambulance." Brady took hold of her hand quickly. "No, water first please! I am supposed to take my medication as soon as this happens". "Oh, okay" she said. The optician literally threw the display screen at the bank manager and ran from there. The bank manager was looking at Brady and was horrified. Brady began to drool saliva from the corner of his mouth. He looked at the bank manager, "Sorry, tissue please." The bank manager looked at him terrified, "Uh, Uh" and turned around to pull some tissues out of the holder. Brady who was clutching the phone to his chest all the time, clicked the mobile twice after placing it just above the digital screen kept on the bank manager's lap. By then the manager turned around with the tissues and he could not take more pictures. Brady was still clutching at his chest and drooling when the manager looked up at him. The optician returned with the water. He took it gratefully and swallowed the pills which he had taken out of a container from his pocket. He took more tissue proffered by the bank manager and wiped his mouth. With a sigh he thanked the two of them. "Thank you I will be better in a few minutes." The optician again offered to call the ambulance. Brady however reassured her, "No it is fine, it happens often. I have been told to take the medicine and not move when it does occur. I go to the hospital every two weeks where they monitor my condition closely. You know the ECG and the lot." The optician relaxed a little bit. She did not have to call the ambulance and create a scene. The business for the whole evening will be jeopardised; if the man was not feeling better and she did have to call the ambulance. "I will move this gentleman away from here and you can relax here for some time." Brady thanked her sincerely.

The optician and the bank manager used the cubicle next door for the remainder of their appointment. Brady received a text message from David. He kept his phone back in his pocket and went to the next cubicle. He knocked to draw their attention to him. He said to the optician, "Thank you for helping me out there." The optician smiled, "No problem. Happy to have been useful." He turned to the bank manager, "Thank you very much to you as well, Sir." The bank manager hurriedly answered, "All I got you, was some tissues?" Brady reassured him, "You know that was a big help. You probably don't realise how big!" The bank manager shrugged his shoulders, "Well, if you say so." Brady raised his fingers to his forehead in salute and left. He was whistling to himself while the optician and the bank manager were feeling sorry for him. They had forgotten about the purpose of his visit!

# CHAPTER 9: NOVEMBER 30th 19:00

The 'Meat and Eat' joint in *Gotrana* was busy. The place was huge, but the popularity of the joint was bigger.

The music was loud and fast. It was a Spanish number. The tempo was such that it will make you get up and dance. There is a science behind playing fast music in eateries. The theory is that when fast music is played, the cooks cooked faster, the waiting staff walked quicker, the people ate faster; and the tables cleared quicker. In a popular establishment, usually people are queued outside. More people eating meant more business. Booming music is a boon for the food industry during peak hours.

The dining tables are in various sizes and shapes covered with colorful table clothes adding to the charm of the place. There were a few tables against the walls which were separated by woven bamboo partitions. This provided the people seated around those tables with a sense of privacy. People with families usually used this place. The large pot planters with tropical plants in the four corners added to the sense of privacy. The loud noise of the music and the people made hearing very difficult. But the men seated around this table were unaware of the noise. Their eyes were focused on Jason. He was still in disguise. As usual he was the first one to arrive and then once the men were seated, he came and joined them. He had been observing them for a good while. They all seemed in high spirits. "Right guys! Listen up. I am glad to see that everyone is excited. Can you report to me your achievements so far?"

David took out a pair of gloves from his pocket with a flourish. "Fingerprints at your service, your highness." Jason inspected the gloves carefully and kept it in his briefcase. "Thank you, David. Excellent work". David replied, "Well Jimmy gets the credit for the fingerprints. I just made the gloves". Jason looked at Jimmy with a smile. Jimmy replied, "It was an interesting task. I enjoyed it." The boys all hooted.

Jason quietened them down. David next took out a small box which when opened revealed a pair of contact lens. "Presenting to you, the eyes of Mr. Williams; courtesy of Brady's heart attack." The boys cheered yet again. Jason laughed. Lucas handed over the gun without any fanfare. Jimmy clapped him on the back. "Good job Lucas" Jason solemnly promised, "I promise that I will try my level best not to use it". Jason quickly hid the gun in his briefcase.

To an outsider it looked like few friends having a good time. But someone who was hearing closely would very soon understand that there was something fishy going down on that table. A woman poked her head in and asked, "You seem to be enjoying your meal boys. Is it okay if I join you? I am very lonely here." The boys were all tensed now. Jimmy looked at Jason to ask as if "Where did this one come from?" But Jason was smiling. He pulled the woman over by his hands and sat her on his lap. "You made your entrance minx. Enough of your dramatics for now! The boys are all shaking like leaves" he chided her tenderly. He looked at the boys and said, "Relax boys. Meet my better half Veronica. She is my childhood sweetheart and my all. But more than that she is the best key maker in town and a lip reader. I escaped from jail because of her specialty at making duplicate keys for handcuffs. Not only that; she can crack safes within ten minutes.

She is the best friend, any man can have." The men were gaping with their eyes wide open.

Veronica stopped Jason's speech by keeping her fingers on his lips. "Sh----- that is enough of your speech. Give the boys a chance". Jimmy is the first person to react. "Well, I am really offended." Veronica quickly reassures him, "You don't have to feel offended. You are still his best friend," Jimmy shook his head like a pouting child, "that's not what I am offended about." Veronica and Jason look at him as if they were asking, "Then?" Jimmy smiled, "He bags the best-looking woman in the country, and I don't know anything about it? It's just not fair".

Veronica laughed happily. Jason smiled, "You have bowled her over". He then looked at Veronica, "This is--." Veronica quietened him down. "Hang on, I know who they are." She pointed at Jimmy, "This gentleman here who has flattered me is Jimmy. Brady, the lonely guy with the blonde beard. David, I like your glasses. They sit very well on your face. Lucas, what's wrong? Why are you frowning?" Lucas shook his head in disbelief. Jason asked him, "What's wrong Lucas?" He answered, "I did not expect a twist like this. I was just thinking that there were only five shares. Now we have to divide it by six."

Jason was annoyed, "No offense Lucas, you still have no idea as to what you are gaining from this enterprise. Why are you worried about six shares? I had already said that whatever we get will be divided equally among all partners. Veronica is also a partner. She deserves an equal share." He turned towards Veronica, "How was your trip?" Veronica silently took a set of keys from her bag. She gave it to Jason. He looked at it carefully. "Just as I had thought." David wanted to know what had he thought? Jason replied, "I am going to lay out the plan as to how we are going to do this job." Lucas sighs, "At last."

Brady looked at him sharply. "Lucas, we had already discussed this. Jason speaks on a need to know basis only? Even Jimmy did not know about Veronica." Jason quietened them down again. He explained patiently to him, "Lucas it is not that I do not trust you; the lesser you know the better. You were not told about Veronica because, I did not want her to be targeted by the police when I escaped. Your harmless banter would be enough for the police to know about her." Lucas was well and truly apologetic. "Sorry Jason, I just always felt left out." David hugged him. "You fool, you were never left out. All of us were treated equally by Jason." Everyone sat and observed the exchange. Jason said, "Now, can we get back to the plan?" Lucas smiled with enthusiasm, "Oh yes, let's get going." Jason smiled, "The plan is to just rob the one person."

Now all their attention was on him solely. He continued, "When I was escaping from prison, I accidentally became a witness to the murder of two people. I felt very vulnerable being in that situation. A few stolen diamonds were the reason for these deaths. I thought that there might be only a small number of rocks but when I saw the diamonds myself, I could not believe my eyes. I had no intention of stealing the diamonds then; but Veronica found out the truth about the murderer and the story behind the murders. He explained to the boys everything that Veronica had seen and heard. Everyone was quiet for some time. Jason took a sip of water.

The men knew in their hearts that they were all thieves and robbers, but they will never play with someone else's life. They knew their limits. They will never breach the unwritten code of honor amongst thieves. Jason looked at them all one by one. He continued "so now the plan is that we will rob Bob 's locker on the 22nd of December." David interjected, "Why not before or after?" Jason replied because 22nd is the last working day for the year so the bank will be busy. "We will not attract unnecessary attention. The diamond auction of the underworld is on the 1st of February; so, the theft hopefully will not be discovered until then. We have to dispose off the diamonds before then". Jason looked around in enquiry. No one had any questions. He breathed deeply and continued. "I opened an account and a locker access in the bank. I can get into the bank on my own legally, no problem". David looked up.

Jason stalled him. "I know David, you don't understand why I made you do all these jobs".

David nodded in exasperation. "I would like to say that everyone needs to earn their keep; which is true". Jason smiled. "But moreover, there are one thousand lockers in five different sections. I can access only mine, so I needed all your help but more so Veronica's!" He continued, "So on the 22nd December, we will commence our work at 1030 and we hope to be on the road by 1130. However, before the big day, I want you guys to swap your roles".

He continued, "So as of tomorrow, David will shadow the bank manager, Jimmy will watch the security guards and Brady will watch the assistant bank manager. Just so that we can ensure that nothing has been missed." Jimmy now frowned whereas Brady smiled. Jason asked Lucas, "Can you organise a van for a few weeks. I will tell you the modifications that you need to make." Lucas was happy with his new task. Even though stealing cars was not his forte, he was looking forward to it.

Jimmy turned towards Veronica. "I am not a curious person by nature Veronica, but I am dying to know how you got the keys?" Veronica actually shuddered. She thought back to the day before Thanks giving.

Bob was seated on the sun lounge beside the swimming pool. This was his resort. A very large concrete building built over a few square kilo-meter. It had everything you desired for during your vacation. A convertible court where you could play any kind of team sports from tennis to Football and a family barbecue area. A kid's swimming pool where the lifeguards kept a careful eye and helped the children who struggled; while their parents chose to do what they wanted. A well-stocked bar with internationally renowned beverages. A large spacious kitchen with two chefs decorated with Michelin stars. Large suites with a living area, bedrooms and ensuite provided added luxury to the package. Room service was available at any time; day or night. A library where the newly published books kept arriving weekly. Whatever else you could think of and desired, it will be at your service at the most within an hour.

Bob was on his own and seated on the lounger. Monty was sitting beside him on another lounger. Monty got all the perks that Bob enjoyed. His driver was the next recipient of all these privileges. Bob rubbed sun lotion on to himself and lay down with his eyes closed. He had a very hearty breakfast and he wanted to give his metabolism a chance to work it out. He will go for a swim later to burn away the excess calories. A few other people were seated on the loungers and some were in the pool.

Sounds of multiple gasps forced Bob to open his eyes. Everyone inclusive of the people who were in the pool were looking at the one spot in the water. Bob did not understand anything. He looked at Monty, who was grinning. Bob imitated the behaviour of the crowd and waited.

In a few seconds a siren emerged from the pool. Bob was astounded first at her beauty and then at her style of emerging from the pool. She looked like the statue of liberty emerging from under the water. Instead of the flame, she had her swimming cap in her hands. Now Bob understood what people we gawking at. They were impressed by the st with which she had dived. She did not r splash. She sliced into the water with minimum amount of water being d

Bob was mesmerised. He kept looking at her. His body became alive with desire. Monty was still grinning at him. He knew that Bob will have a very beautiful thanksgiving now! He himself will pick someone up later. Any person who caught his eyes and was willing. At least Bob was sorted. The driver was already holed in with someone. Now they can all have a highly satisfactory Thanksgiving Day.

The siren who emerged from the pool did a
ˡaps and then came and sat in the lounger
Bob. She rubbed the excess water off
owel and smeared some lotion on
ch movement was designed to be
hen lay down on the lounger and
He h. Bob kept staring at her.
she was
gawking?" beauties in his life time, but
al. "Have you finished
d. "I don't appreciate

people staring at me when I am trying to sleep". Bob was embarrassed. He felt like a small child who got caught with his hands in a jar of candy. But he could not stop himself from retorting back. "People who pretend to sleep in sun loungers actually want others to admire them." She looked at him in disgust. Bob laughed.

She got up with as much decorum as she c̸
muster and swaggered away. Bob's cu̸
was perked up. He looked at Mon̸
smiled. He got up from his lounger an̸
towards the reception. Bob lay do̸
eyes closed. Monty will need tim̸
There is no point in him being ̸
that was not his style. The ha̸
the tastier was the meat.

In the evening, Bob was ̸tting at the bar. His employee, the bar at̸nder fixed his drink exactly the way he liked it. Bob sat quietly and enjoyed his drinks. The bar attender moved away to cater to the other customers. The bar is usually full at this time of the evening. Tonight, was no exception. A few couples were on the dance floor swaying to the soft romantic music emerging effortlessly from the speakers hidden in discrete corners.

A person came and sat on one of the bar stools. She ordered a drink, "May, I have a St. Adams please? The bar tender was regretful, "Sorry madam, we do not have St. Adams in stock. If you care to choose something else? I will get your favourite drink within the hour". Veronica was disappointed. "Oh, what else do you have? The bar tender answered that there was everything else. She replied, "okay give me a---"

"A martini" Bob interjected. Veronica turned towards him and looked at his drink curiously. Bob responded, "It's not that bad you know?" Veronica just shrugged. The bar tender was under pressure now. He understood what was happening. A dance! A cat and mouse game! Bob was waiting for his chance to pounce on whoever this beauty was. He prepared a Martini which would surpass all the other Martini's he had ever made. He placed it reverently in front of Veronica. She took a sip and closed her eyes. She savoured the taste that hit her mouth. Her palate came alive with sensations of olive and lime. "This is good!" She exclaimed. "On the house" said Bob. She thanked him and kept sipping her drink. She took her time to finish her drink. Bob ordered another one for her. "So, you are trying to get me drunk" she remarked to him. Bob smiled, "Let's just say that I want to know about you. Apart from arising from the pool like a mermaid; what else are you good at?"

Veronica gave a tinkling laugh. "You can definitely flatter women". They kept quiet for a good while. She looked around the bar with casual interest. "A nice place. Whoever owns it is filthy rich." Bob looked at her. "Allow me to introduce you to the owner." He bowed. "You! You are the owner of this place?" She asked in disbelief. "Mmm, you must be loaded?" Veronica commented. Bob replied modestly, "Yes I can manage to survive." Veronica looked at him and then they both burst out laughing. They kept chatting for a good while. Around midnight, they both got up to go and staggered up the stairs. "I will escort you to your room." Bob offered. He had learnt from Monty that her room was right beside his. It will be an interesting night. "Thanks...ss" she slurred.

The bar tender was watching. "The bird is in the net" he murmured to himself and turned back to his own job. The bar did not close during the night. It just became comparatively quieter at the time. Bob walked up to the floor where Veronica's room was housed. He had acted surprised when she told him the suite number. "Your place or mine?" He asked. Veronica laughingly accused him. "You, you are trying to get me into your bed, aren't you?" Bob rubbed her cheek tenderly and whispered. "You want it as badly as I do." Veronica smiled. Bob held her hand and pulled her gently to his room. Monty and the driver are right behind them. Bob signalled to them to stop. They had anticipated the events. They sat down on the couch in the seating area on the landing. They called for room service. It will be a while before they went to their bed.

In the room, Bob and Veronica are seated on a couch. Bob pulled her close to him to kiss her. Veronica pushed him away. "You are a terrible host. You have not offered me a drink yet." Bob looked at her. "Oh, sweetheart! Do you really want one now? I have other means of intoxication." She laughed. "Then let me get on a double high." She staggered to the fridge and opened it. It was a well-stocked fridge. She took out two beers and poured it into two glasses. Her ring on the right hand had a lid with a photo. She had the picture of a red rose on the lid. "Waiting for the picture of the right man." She had explained to Bob at the bar earlier in the evening.

She flipped open the lid and some powder fell out of it straight into the glass. If he drank this, he will have temporary amnesia. When he wakes up, he will not remember the drama that was going to unfold now. She came back to the couch and offered him the pint glass. "Cheers, to a fantastic time" he cried. "Cheers" she replied with a smile. They both slugged their beer. Bob was semi reclined on the couch now. His hold on the glass loosened slowly. At one stage he let go. She was watching his every move carefully and caught the glass before it crashed to the floor. She pulled him so that he could lie flat on the couch. "Oh my! He is heavy." She then lay down beside him and fumbled with his coat as if she was groping for him. He was snoring now. She found his set of keys and noiselessly pulled it out. Her handbag was lying on the floor beside her. It was just within reach. Bob coughed and stopped snoring for a while.

Veronica held her breath. "I am going to fail Jason" she thought to herself. Bob began to snore again. "Hmph, he suffers from sleep apnea. He should see his doctor". But she knew that men like him will never expose their weakness. She lay still and noiselessly took out a large bar of soap from her bag. It was slightly moist. She carefully cast the impression of all the keys that were on the key ring. She stayed lying like that for a little while.

She then slowly got up and walked to the loo. She washed the keys, used the rest room and came out. Her heart was in her mouth. Bob was sitting up and looking at her intently. He asked gruffly, "What are you doing?" Veronica went back to the couch. She rubbed the nape of his neck. She helped him get out of his jacket. "What? Am I not allowed to use the rest room?" Did you miss me that much?" she asked him.

She made him drink some more of the remaining beer. He relaxed and lay down. She also lay down beside him and began to rub his cheeks. He was asleep again now. Soft gentle snoring could be heard after a while. Veronica breathed a sigh of relief. She kept the keys gently on the bed beside him. The jacket was lying crumpled under him now. He will think that the keys dropped on the side accidentally.

She undid the fly of his trouser. She turned away from him but pulled down his underwear. She then covered him with a blanket. She turned back to check if he was descent. She got up and picked up the glasses. She drained the rest of the drink down the sink.

She rinsed the glasses and poured the remaining beer from the cans. She had been careful to save some. "Just enough to coat the glass again." Jason had instructed her. "Better not leave a clue," She rinsed the sink for good measure. She picked up her handbag and looked at Bob once more. He was fast asleep. The snoring had slowed down to a wheeze. In a while it will stop. He will sleep soundly after that. She came out to the lounge. The driver was asleep, but Monty was sitting and watching television. He shook the driver awake. "He is fast asleep," she told them.

Monty nodded his head and signalled for her to wait. The driver had his sleep laden eyes on her. He knew the drill. Usually the women stayed the night. But some of them were married and needed to be back home. Some just could not take it any more from him, so they left. She might be the third type. She was in the bar when he had searched her room. He did not find anything that told him that she was attached. Her boarding pass was from a small town in a remote part of Canada.

Monty had come out from Bob's suite by now. He nodded his head again and Veronica gently walked in to her room. "Goodnight gentlemen!" "She is a lady" thought Monty. "Most women left the place very untidy and Bob exposed; but this woman had covered his master properly afterwards. On the other hand, her hands trembled as she inserted the card to the door lock. She was not out of the woods yet. She opened the door, entered the room and closed the door behind her. She leaned on the door and took a long breath. She had no idea as to how long she had been standing.

She kept looking out of the peep hole for a good long time. The men had gone inside now. It was all quiet. She waited for another thirty minutes. She then picked up her bags which were already packed. She vacated the room and checked out at reception. She caught the four O' clock flight to Washington, then to Vancouver. She kept flying and traveling with alternate modes of transport between and within America and Canada for the whole day. She was exhausted. This morning, she caught the flight home. As soon as she got in; she began to prepare the keys. She then came straight to the 'Meat and Eat' joint.

The boys were looking at her open mouthed. Lucas was very impressed. "You have been to the lion's den and back!" She looked at him with gratitude for believing her. Jason would not have allowed her to go had he not trusted her; both her capabilities and her virtue. But coming from Lucas who was described as the 'Doubting Thomas' it was a big deal. Now she knew that she had earned their respect and undeniable trust forever! It could have been easy for them to think less of her and supply unnecessary and dirty details from the figment of their own personal imagination. But Lucas had echoed the sentiment of the group. She had passed the test and had been accepted.

Jason had watched the reaction of the men as Veronica had related the story. Jason sighed with relief, he had to risk Veronica losing her respect. No need to worry now. He smiled, "I have to bring my angel to bed. Look she is half asleep already." Veronica opened her eyes at the mention of her name and smiled. Everyone said their goodbyes and then Jason and Veronica left the joint. The men continued with their meal and their conversation. Unlike Jason, they were going to go back to the dreary old dormitory.

# CHAPTER 10: DECEMBER 22nd 10:00

Lucas got into the van in the morning. He made one last check of everything before commencing on this adventure. Hopefully this will set them up for life.

Brady had taught him how to steal a vehicle. He had gone to a junk yard and got the most dirty and old looking van available in working condition in that scrap. He then had re-organised the other vehicles in such a manner that no one will be able to detect that a van was missing. He ignited the engine by rubbing together the two wires. He extricated it out of the compound without being detected. He then brought it out to the deserted warehouse, where he had made the gun.

He gave the van a lick of black paint. He stuck a commercial sticker advertising a faux wedding planner company. He stocked up on few stickers representing different companies of the same measurement. It was a precautionary measure. Just in case they had to make a quick getaway.

Even a plain black van will draw the attention of someone. It is better to change stickers and number plates in case there was a problem. He also had prepared about twenty false number plates. He kept them within reach in the boot. Next, he stocked up on food and drinks. Jason had vetoed on alcohol of any kind, which a bummer! But he understood that they all needed a clear head. He then fitted a wooden panel on one wall and Jimmy set up a monitor and a receiver inside the panel. The van was good to go now. It just needed to be serviced.

Brady did a thorough servicing of the van. He had learnt a lot about vehicles during his stay and work with Peter. He changed the engine oil, break oil and the tyres and the tubes, He even installed new bulbs, changed the battery, replaced the oil for the engine, changed the brake pads and refilled the water in the radiator. He knew that Jason was paranoid about cars not being in perfect working order. This stemmed from the fact that he had landed in jail in the first place because of a stalled car. 'Once bitten, twice shy,' he thought to himself. Looking at the van now; no one will think that it came from a scrap yard. The van was shining and bright new. The men had put in a lot of effort in bringing it up to a high standard.

Lucas was in *Grantageona*, which was twenty minutes from *Clapa Gopolini*. They had vacated the city of *Gotrana*. Jason was spending his time in *Clapa Gopolini*. He had booked another room on the same floor with a better view of the bank. He used his current false passport for identification this time. He had paid occasional visits to Veronica as much as possible. He needed to make sure that the diamonds were not going anywhere!

He knew that all of them being in one place for a long duration will be dangerous. They were all at risk of landing back in the prison. They had broken the conditions of their parole. But he had the most to loose on every account.

Heaving a heavy sigh, Lucas got into the van and took the highway to *Clapa Gopolini*. He had to be there for twenty-five past ten. He knew that he had sufficient time. He was relaxed because his job for now was over. He will be the getaway driver. The rest will be only beginning their jobs now.

He reached *Clapa Gopolini* without incidence and parked two blocks away in an alley. He was right on time. Brady was seated on a bench outside the bank reading a newspaper. It was a cold morning, but Brady was sweating. "Brady here, operation glitter initiated" he had mentioned the password into the ear piece, signalling the commencement of the job. Lucas heard this on conference call as had been decided by Jason. He smiled to himself in anticipation.

David took a deep breath. It was his turn now. He went into the coffee shop when he saw Tony coming out of the bank. He knew that Tony will spend exactly five minutes for smoking the cigarette. He was happy that it was Tony he had to trick. It should be relatively easy.    He had understood from his observations that, Tony was a happy go lucky man. David joined the queue and ordered coffee. He went to the counter and began mixing the sugar just as Tony would have prepared it. He was observing Tony all the time. Now Tony had nearly finished paying. David took his handkerchief out of his trouser pocket. A fifty Euro note fell to the floor. David continued to stir his coffee as if he had not noticed it. Tony turned around after collecting the coffee and walked over to the milk and sugar counter.

He saw the note on the floor. He looked around and then looked at David. He kept his coffee cup on the counter. He then bent down and picked up the note from the floor. He looked at David again. "Is this your's mate?" He asked. David turned around to face him. He was startled. He looked at the note wistfully.    He regretfully said, "No mate, finder's keepers." Tony smiled in relief and kept the money in his pocket. "A jackpot for Christmas," he said. They both smiled at each other. Tony went out with his purchase and David stayed there. He looked at the time. It was ten thirty. "David here, trap set" he called out happily into the ear piece.

Lucas looked at the monitor in the van. He smiled. He could see the visual of the bank a few yards away swimming up and down on the monitor matching with Tony's footsteps. "Success," he said into the phone. He knew that all of them were smiling at the receiving end. David now began to stir the coffee which Tony had brought and kept on the counter. Tony had forgotten that he did not add sugar to his coffee in the excitement of seeing the money. David prepared this coffee in the same manner and brought it out of the coffee shop.

Meanwhile, Tony was walking towards the bank. He was on cloud nine. He took a sip of coffee from his cup and kept it back on the tray. He thought regretfully that he should have bought one more coffee. No worries, he can get another treat at lunch time! He now had the money to buy the gift that Clara wanted for Christmas.

"Oh no boys, interference with the visual!" Lucas cried out. David quickly asked, "What's the problem?" Lucas answered in a panicky voice. "Looks like he turned the camera face of the cup inwards. Now all I can see is a hairy chest." David groaned, "What do I do now?"

Jason's voice came through the microphone, "Stay there David. Let's wait." Lucas agreed, "He is still a good few steps away from the bank. He might take another sip." Lucas unconsciously crossed his fingers. They all waited anxiously. Lucas' voice came through, "Okay now David, you can proceed as planned." David let out his breath. He kept walking towards the van. He was glad that they did not have to alter their plan any further.

"Jimmy! Are you ready?" Asked Lucas. Jimmy replied yes and took out a paper and pen. Lucas called out 'CZ 22453'. Jimmy quickly scribbled it down. He met David and took the coffee holder from him. Jimmy waited a little distance away from the bank. Tony went into the security guard's cabin after opening the door. He said to Javier, "I am giving you a treat today." Javier turned to look at him in enquiry and smiled, "Did you get a special bonus?" Tony answered back with a grin, "Something like that." Lucas smiled when he heard this jovial conversation. While they were both engrossed in their casual chat, neither of them were looking at the screen. Lucas called out, "Jimmy now." Jimmy answered, "Yes I am going in." By this time, David was comfortably seated in the warmth of the van beside his brother. They both did a high five with their hands. They were safe now. They knew that Jason had sequenced the job in this pattern; so that they could escape together if a problem cropped up!

Brady's voice was on the verge of crying as he entered the conversation. "Lads, I can't see Denise. It is twenty to eleven now." Everyone panicked at their ends. There was no turning back! Surely, she was not out sick. They prayed that she had not taken her holidays. They had seen her yesterday. She had come in to work. Jason quietly spoke into his phone. "Don't panic Brady. Let's wait. She is only five minutes late. It is quarter to eleven now? Brady you can go and wait in the coffee shop". Brady replied that he will walk to the coffee shop now.

*Clive Dev*

Lucas reassured him. "Don't worry mate. She will arrive. We are destined to live a happy life." Everyone smiled nervously in their positions. Lucas had changed after hearing Veronica's account of the locker key theft. Good! He needed someone to shake him awake from his fantasyland.

Meanwhile, Jimmy had opened the side gate by now. He walked into the security guard's cabin. He saw Javier sitting in his chair but was already face down on the table. Tony turned around at the noise from the door, "Who are you ma---n? His vision was blurred. He slurred in his speech and then he too went face down on the table. Jimmy quickly moved Tony's coffee cup out of the way. He was delighted that he had a really steady hand. Otherwise the coffee that he was holding in his hand, would have spilled and made a mess!

228

He looked at the display monitors. The pictures from all the cameras were feeding into a hard disk on the computer. He disconnected all the terminals except the one that fed pictures from the foyer of the bank. But he forfeited the command for the computer to store the memory. He then rewound the tape for the last ten minutes and fed it into the hard disk on rewind. He had erased the memory of the previous five minutes; where he would have been filmed entering the side door. Jimmy spoke into his microphone. "Jimmy here, scenery intact."

Jason thanked him but he was becoming nervous now. He cannot move till Denise gets handed the drugged coffee. Jimmy reassured him. "Don't worry. I can see her use the side door from the foyer." He asked Brady who was waiting in the coffee shop, if he was ready and Brady replied yes. "But there is a long queue." Brady got into the queue and ordered two coffees. Once he had collected it, he went to the sugar counter. He began to prepare the coffee just as he had seen her do before. Another person purchased their beverage and left without coming to the counter.

Brady was thankful for this. Three is always a crowd. Denise now approached the Deli staff. Who remarked casually, "Denise, you are late today." Denise smiled and replied, "Yes Cynthia, it is very busy. More people are trying to send money home for Christmas." Cynthia replied, "Christmas is good for us as well. We can make up for the holiday season" Denise smiled, "Christmas is good either way. All right, I am late. Talk soon." She went up to the counter but did not keep the coffee cups down. Instead, she placed them on a holder but did not let go. She then picked up the paper towels with her free hand.

Brady was at a loss. He was not able to switch the cups. Neither did he want to panic the boys. Denise folded the tissue papers in her hand and walked out. Brady waited for a few seconds. He had not anticipated this move. He will fail all of them now! This job was his only responsibility. For the whole month, everything had been working fine. But not when it actually matters. He came out of the shop in a panic. He was undecided about his next move. He had not said anything to the lads yet. He smiled at the sight he saw when he came out of the coffee shop. He can see Denise standing outside the coffee shop keeping a cigarette in her mouth. She is searching for a light. She had left the coffee cups on the table beside her. Brady kept his coffee holder beside the coffee holder that she had already kept on the table. He lit her cigarette for her. "Thanks" she replied and smiled. He had in the meantime switched her coffee holder with his. "Welcome" he smiled and walked away.

Denise took two puffs of her cigarette and then threw it in to the bin. She lifted up the coffee tray from the table and walked hurriedly towards the bank. "I am already late," she murmured to herself. Brady was grinning now as he spoke into the microphone, "Brady here, the damsel in distress is rescued". He went back to the bench outside the bank and resumed his position.

Jason looked at the clock. Exactly eleven in the morning! They were running ten minutes late according to their schedule. He waited for five more minutes and then he began to walk to the bank. He took big strides and reached the bank in two minutes. This was the last step to a glorious future. There was no turning back!

Whatever happened after this, he could not deceive his friends who had come with him this far. He went up to the receptionist. "Hello, I would like to access my locker please." The receptionist looked at him and replied apologetically, "Good morning sir, It will be a few minutes. It is very busy today." Jason thanked her. She asked him for his bank card. "May I take your card please? Jason handed over the card to her. "Sure," he said. She handed over the card machine to him and he keyed in the Personal Identification Number. She thanked him politely.

Once the PIN was accepted; she said to him, "Please take a seat near that door Mr. Shears. One of the managers will come and escort you shortly," Jason thanked her and walked to the chair near the door. He sat down quietly. He looked around the bank in curiosity. It was very busy. There was a long queue for the ATM. Another queue to the printing machine. Many people were awaiting their turn at the foreign exchange counter.

The bank will be closed from tomorrow for Christmas. He had heard that the people of *Clapa Gopolini* celebrated their Christmas in style. Other than the emergency services, every other establishment will be closed. The first working week of the new year will be the next working day in this city.

Jason saw someone which made him feel suddenly terrified. He could see a policeman walking in to the bank with an envelope in his hand. Jason panicked. "Why did you have to appear now?" he mentally questioned the man. "Have you nothing better to do today?" he lamented. While he was getting worked up, the bank manager came to the door and called out his name. "Mr. Shears!" Jason was dumbfounded. He was in a state of paralysis. His tongue was stuck to the roof of the mouth. He could not move. He had eyes for the policeman only. The bank manager looked at him in exasperation. "It is already busy," he thought. "what was he doing?" "Mr. Shears!" He tried to call him again.

The policeman went to one of the ATM with the envelope. He inserted his card and took out some money. The men were all nervous. They heard the bank manager calling Jason's name. But they couldn't see what was happening with the exception of Jimmy. Jason still did not react. Jimmy was torn; he did not want to startle Jason and raise any alarm. Things may turn pear shaped. "Mr. Shears" the bank manager was impatient now. "J" Jason came out of his trance at Jimmy's voice and turned very quickly towards the bank manager. "Sorry, I was dreaming." The bank manager laughed, "It's all right Mr. Shears. No better place to dream about making millions". Jason nervously laughed in response.

The bank manager allowed him to pass through the door. Jason waited inside the door; till the bank manager joined him. The metal door clanged with a loud noise. This clanging echoed in all the phone receivers; bringing them all back to the memory of the prison. Jason began to suffocate. Jimmy could understand him, "Breathe slowly" he said. He could hear him rasping through the receiver. They entered the corridor. A door marked 'staff lounge' will appear in the corner. Jason thought to himself. He was trying to keep himself distracted. Beside the lounge is the restroom. Denise' room was at the end of the corridor. Jason knew all of this from his repeated visits to the bank. The locker area began after her room. Five sections of two hundred lockers each. He clutched his briefcase tightly to himself in stress. The bank manager called out, "Denise! Are you ready?" "Yes, Mr. Williams, just a---- minute," a slurred voice called out. Jason relaxed. The drug was working. Finally, a smile touched the outline of his lips. They both waited at the end of the corridor. Denise came out of her door. She was a bit slow in her reaction time. Jason looked at her carefully. Her pupils were dilated. "Hello Mr. Shears, how aa—rre you?" Jason replied, "I am very well, thank you." "Even better now that you are drugged," he thought to himself. Together they walked towards the corridor holding the lockers. Another exit door closed! Jason's panic increased ten-fold.

Denise was now really unwell. She knew that she will fall. It will be embarrassing. "Excuse me gentlemen, I will join you in a minute." She turned back and entered another corridor within that space. Jason observed her progress. He then turned towards the bank manager. He kept a careful eye on him. The bank manager was also showing signs of swaying. Suddenly, the bank manager's legs gave in. Jason quickly held on to the bank manager's arm. He slid him down with the help of his own torso and sat him on the floor. The bank manager's eyes were open, but his vision was blurring. He leant on the wall with Jason's help and then his eyes closed over. Jason knew that it is just the three of them here in this area of the bank. But he looked around carefully. He cocked his ears to one side and listened carefully. No noise, of any approaching footsteps could be heard.

Jason took a deep breath. Now even Jimmy couldn't see him. They just had to wait till they hear him speak again. Until then, it was all guess work. Jason took out the gloves with Denise' finger print from his pocket and placed it on top of the scanner on the wall. The panel opened and the eye scanner popped out. Jason's eyes were already fitted with the lens. David had manufactured the lens according to the structure of the iris of the Bank manager's eyes; but it had the strength of Jason's vision. This meant that he could see properly.

Jason thanked David mentally. He aligned his eye in line with the scanner. The vault door swung open. He had memorised the number of Bob's lockers and directly moved to that compartment. The door slid closed behind him. Now even Jason had no clue as to what was happening outside. He had timed himself before this. He needed two and a half minutes at the maximum to finish the job.

11:20:00 He inserted the key to one of Bob's lockers. The door slid open. He could see a few papers in the box. He searched the locker with his gloved hands. He did not find anything remotely resembling what he was looking for. He closed the locker door and locked it with the key.

11:21:00 Jason looked for the other locker. He knew exactly where it was. The compartments although separate had the same design. He opened the second locker and slid the door open. He could see the briefcase straight away. He picked it up. He opened it and looked at the diamonds. He gasped at the glitter. Jimmy heard him and understood. "J" he whispered. Jason became alert. He picked up his own briefcase. It was the same color; it also had the picture of 'a green-eyed monster'. He quickly rubbed down the briefcase with the gloves. There will be no prints now. Then he kept his briefcase into Bob's locker. The briefcase with the diamond was still open. He closed it and picked it up.

11:22:30 He reached the door and pushed the exit switch on the wall. The door slid open. He peeped out and looked around. The bank manager was still there on the floor; only more slouched! No other noise could be heard. He came out of the vault. The door slid closed again.

He took a deep breath and went to the corridor which Denise had taken. He found her in a restroom. She was lying on the floor. He approached her and called out her name softly. "Denise---". At the other end, each one of them was waiting with bated breath. There was no response. Jason went nearer. He took out a nasal spray from the pocket of his jacket. He sprayed it on her nose and quickly walked out. He approached the bank manager and sprayed the drug to his nose as well. The bank manager jolted out of his unconsciousness. Jason was glad that he was able to quickly hide the nasal spray back into his pocket. He scolded David mentally. He had not told him the response time of the drug, "If I get out of this alive; I am going to kill him," he promised to himself.

Jason modulated his voice to project alarm. "Mr. Williams! Are you all right?" The bank manager was confused, "W--- what happened Mr. Shears?" Jason replied calmly, "I don't know Mr. Williams but, you suddenly began to lose consciousness. I prevented you from falling and sat you down on the floor." The bank manager was embarrassed. He tried to stand up and floundered. Jason quickly supported him; the bank manager was grateful. He stood up with Jason's help and tidied himself. Footsteps could be heard in the corridor.

Denise was looking as immaculate as ever. "Sorry gentlemen, I needed a bit longer than necessary" she said to them. She had no idea as to how long she had been out. She also took some time to freshen up as well. She did not like her reflection in the mirror when she had looked at it. "Everyone will be curious on seeing my appearance," she thought to herself. Both the men smiled reassuringly, then looked at each other and winked.

The bank manager was suddenly very professional and smiled, "Okay Denise, let's get Mr. Shears sorted." He did not know what had happened to him; but he was back in command now. They moved towards the vault and the bank manager and Denise opened the vault after following the protocol.

11:27:00 Jason was now in the compartment where his locker was situated. He opened his locker and emptied the contents. He spent some time. He then closed the door and came out of the compartment. He looked at the two of them. "All done, Mr. Williams." he said happily. The boys at the other end continue to hold their breath. It was not over yet, they know. The bank manager replied, "All right then. Let's go." The three of them reached outside Denise' room. She wished a merry Christmas to Jason, "Merry Christmas, Mr. Shears." He wished her the same in return. Denise went back into her room thoughtfully. She had no clue as to what had happened to her. She sat down and took a big sigh. "Its good that no one had seen her," she thought to herself.

When they arrived near the staff lounge, Jason turned to the bank manager and asked, "Mr. Williams, is it all right to use the toilet quickly?" There was a toilet in the foyer but after Jason's 'assistance' in the vault, the bank manager could not deny his request. "Oh absolutely!" he said. Jason thanked him and went into the toilet. He went through the motions of relieving himself. He then turned the tap on in full force. He took out two used coffee cups from inside his jacket and opened the pedal bin. He could see two coffee cups inside the bin. He picked them up in his right hand and dropped the cups from his left hand into the bin. The bin closed softly. He spent a few minutes in the toilet and then he came out. He thanked the bank manager who smiled and escorted him out. He opened the exit door for him and allowed Jason to pass. Jason once outside turned around and shook the bank manager's hand. "Merry Christmas," he said and added, "mind yourself" with a wink. The bank manager was flustered, and his cheeks became red. He mumbled something hurriedly and closed the door behind him. Jason smiled in glee. He turned around and walked through the foyer aiming for the exit.

11:30:00 "Mr. Shears, could you stop for a moment please!" a voice called out. Jason stopped in his tracks. He was like a deer that was caught in the headlights. The boys apart from Jimmy were worse as they had no clue.

"Mr. Shears," the voice called out again. He turned around in what seemed like hours to him. It was the reception staff calling out to him. He smiled wanly at her. "Mr. Shears, you forgot your hat" she said to him and was pointing to a hat on the desk. Jason smiled a very broad smile. His shoulder sagged in relief. He nearly genuflects in thanks. He picked up the hat and walked out of the bank.

11:32:00 Jason walked straight to the van which had been slowly moving to the bank as each step took place. Jason knocked on the door. Lucas let him in. Jason literally fell on to the seat. David thumped him on the bank which helped him ease his breathing. "The stars are shining," said Jason with a smile when he was able to get his breath back. It was not over yet! Jimmy was waiting in the security guard's office. He now replaced the connections back into the original positions. He checked the system again. Everything was working fine now. He picked up the drugged cups and left the 'good' coffee cups in place. He took Tony's hand and kept his fingers on top of the 'enter' key on the keyboard of the computer. He then got out and closed the door behind him. He then took out the nasal spray.

He sprayed the drug from the nasal spray through the exhaust vent from the outside of the cabin. If he sprayed directly, the men will wake up suddenly. Using the vent will give him time to escape. His image will not be recorded on the camera. He was depending on Tony to switch the system back on. He came out of the bank through the side gate. When the outer side door clanged shut, the security guard, Tony woke up with a start.

His fingers reflexively hit the 'enter' key of the key board. He looked at the monitor and saw that all was functioning well. At the same time,

Jimmy's voice cried in relief, "Action reset". Tony was looking at the screen as Jimmy was walking by on the footpath. Tony had no clue, how he fell asleep. He scrolled the screen and looked at the recording. Everything was fine. He relaxed. He woke up Javier and gave him a hard time; but did not confess his own guilt!

11:33:00 Brady heard Jimmy's voice and got up from his post. He had been waiting for Jimmy to spell out the golden words which will let him get up from there. He looked around cautiously once more and then walked to the van. The van has been slowly traveling in the opposite direction now with every code word that was spelt out. Brady walked faster. He saw the van at the next intersection of the road. He began to walk faster.

11:36:00 He knocked on the door of the van. "Password please" came a chorus from the inside. Lucas looked out from the side window and grinned. Brady looked at him with a wide smile, "Mission accomplished". The door of the van magically opened. He got in. Everyone backslapped him as he found a place to sit. Lucas laughed and sped away on the highway.

## CHAPTER 11: December 31st 17:00

The boys were somewhere in a tropical island. They were playing with a beach ball. They are well tanned and looked healthy. A car approached the beach car park. Everyone turned around in anticipation mixed with anxiety. Suddenly Jimmy hooted. Jason and Veronica got out of the car accompanied by cheers from the boys. Everyone ran up to them. They lifted Jason up in celebration. They folded Veronica in to a group hug.

The boys were delighted that Jason was safe now. After confiscating the diamonds; as robbing will not be the correct word to use now, Jason had got out of the van on the highway. He had asked the boys to proceed to an agreed destination. He was going to collect Veronica who had moved out of *Gotrana* and was hiding in a remote village in France. If

Bob found out that his diamonds were gone and he saw Veronica in the same town; it will not have taken him long to connect the dots. She had moved out of the rented bungalow, the previous day of the 'accidental heist'.

Now they were all seated around the dinner table. Laughter and chat was very loud. Everyone was in high spirits with the exception of Lucas. Jason looked at him in anger. "Lucas, what is wrong now?" Lucas was startled at Jason's angry voice. He looked at him for a few minutes and then laughed out loud. Everyone was now looking at him. It was beyond their comprehension. Lucas had never been so cheerful. Lucas controlled his laughter with difficulty. Holding his tummy, he asked Jason, "What do you think will be Bob's reaction? Jason looked at him in terror. Understanding suddenly dawned on him. He laughed, "You have to wait until the 1st of February to know what happens. His reaction will be the same as

Tommy when he had seen Bob on the trawler."
Everyone laughed. Jason continued, "He will
very soon find out to his horror 'what goes
around; comes around.'"

On the 31st of January, Bob went to the bank
in the morning. He waited his turn for access
to the locker. When the bank manager called
him, he smiled widely and went in. He shook
the manager's hand in gusto. His happiness
knew no bounds. He was there to retrieve the
diamonds; in preparation for the black-market
auction.

The three of them walked to the vault as per
protocol. Bob went in to the compartment that
held his locker. He opened the locker which
contained the diamonds. He smiled in
anticipation and opened the briefcase; his
smile died a sudden death. The briefcase was
stuffed with plenty of crumpled papers and

small rocks. There was a colorful card on the top. "Tit for Tat" it said with a smile.

*Clive Dev*

STORIES COLLECTION

We are a team of story/script writers of different genre focused on Book Publication and film production. Some are the Glimpses / Narratives of our creations. Our projects are subject to intellectual copy right. If you like our Narratives and if you are interested in film production.

Please visit: clivestorycreations.com

# True Colors: the accidental heist

CPSIA information can be obtained
at www.ICGtesting.com
Printed in the USA
LVHW041550280519
619299LV00003B/688/P

9 781793 884732